FIC Moo   8 8 0 0 1 3
Moore, Emily.
Something to count on

FIC Moo   8 8 0 0 1 3
Moore, Emily.
Something to count on

9.95

TITLE

DATE DUE	BORROWER'S NAME	ROOM NUMBER
	3-B	
FEB 15 1988	Sarah S	3-B
APR 25 1988	Brown	
JUN 20 89	Colette O.	3-D

Something To Count On

■ ■ ■ ■ ■ ■ ■ ■ ■ ■

Something To Count On

by Emily Moore

A Unicorn Book

E. P. DUTTON   NEW YORK

Library of Congress Cataloging in Publication Data

Moore, Emily.   Something to count on.
(A Unicorn Book)
SUMMARY: Ten-year-old Lorraine's behavior problems
at school are aggravated by her family situation and
eased by an understanding new teacher.
[1. Divorce—Fiction. 2. School Stories]   I. Title.
PZ7.M7834So 1980 [Fic]   79-23277 ISBN: 0-525-39595-4

Published in the United States by E. P. Dutton, Inc., New York

Published simultaneously in Canada by Clarke,
Irwin & Company Limited, Toronto and Vancouver

Editor: Emilie McLeod   Designer: Stacie Rogoff

Printed in the U.S.A.
10 9 8 7 6 5 4 3 2

For my father and Charles, with love

1

■ ■ ■ ■ ◙

"Where's my father?" I asked Mr. Al, the man Daddy worked for in the auto repair shop. I looked and saw that the blue overalls Daddy wore so he wouldn't get all greasy were hanging on a hook. Daddy was nowhere around. And this was the second time today I'd been here.

"Girl, I ain't seen your daddy all day. And he left me here with all this work." Mr. Al took a tire off a brown car and rolled it to the back of the shop. "I'm busy. You can't wait," he said when he saw I was sitting there with my wet towel.

"When he comes back, tell him, I . . ."

"Yeah. Yeah. Yeah." He waved me off and disappeared into another room.

I went home. It was so hot, I walked kind of slow. But when I got to my building, I ran up the stairs and busted through the door.

"Don't slam that door," Ma said. But I already did. Ma was wearing lipstick and she wasn't sweating. She looked like there was company. "Look at you," she said. "You got that new shirt all wet." Ma took the wet towel from me and told me to change my clothes. "Carrying these wet things under your arm. Why don't you use that knapsack of yours?" She picked up the knapsack from the bathroom floor.

"It's only for important stuff," I said. "Not for clothes." I must've told Ma that a million times, but she never listens.

While I changed, Ma rinsed out my bathing suit.

"I swim almost good now," I said.

"You're being careful?" Ma asked. She hung the bathing suit on the clothesline over the bathtub.

"Yes, ma'am." I sounded sweet.

Ma raised her eyebrow. "What've you been up to anyway?"

"Nothing. Looking for Daddy. And you know what? He disappeared."

Ma sighed. "Honestly. He's home. . . . He's here."

"Home? This time of day?"

"Lorraine—" Ma grabbed my arm before I could run to find Daddy. "I have to talk to you."

"What I do now?" I was always being blamed for something. Even some things I didn't do. But I shut up until Ma actually blamed me for doing something wrong.

"Nothing. Yet. Go in my bedroom," she said. "Jason's already there."

Ma was acting strange, sort of like the time Grandpa was dying. She and Daddy explained to us about dying. Something had to be wrong now. It must be Daddy. I broke from Ma and raced to their bedroom.

Daddy was sitting on the side of the bed. Jason was

2

bouncing on his lap. I ran over to him and hugged him. The hair on his face scratched me. It never did before.

Jason pointed at me and said, "You in trouble."

The one bad thing about my brother, the pip-squeak, is that he is a pain in the neck. The best thing about him is he never stays home. He's always playing next door with his friend, Julio. I hope Julio never moves away. I licked my tongue at him.

"Stop, you two," said Daddy.

"He started it," I said. "Why we in here anyway?" Their room was hot.

Ma sat down in a chair. She held out one arm to me. Her eyes shined like two black jewels. "Remember how I told you we'd always be a family?"

I nodded slowly.

"No matter where we go?" she asked.

"We moving?" Jason asked, staring at Daddy.

"I want to move," I said.

Ma squeezed my hands. "No. Nobody's moving. I mean . . . Look, see . . ." She glanced over at Daddy, then looked back at me. "A lot of times, two people, who loved each other—they can be mothers and fathers, aunts and uncles, grandparents, or people we don't know—they find out things about each other. They can't be happy living together anymore."

I think I knew what Ma meant. And I was afraid to believe it was true. But it had to be. Lately, all I hear at night is their fussing. Daddy would storm out of the house and come back real late. Ma would be crying in their bedroom.

"Are you listening?" Ma asked.

I nodded.

3

"They find out they can't be happy living together anymore."

I looked at Daddy. He said, "They might still care for each other." His eyes blinked real fast, and they looked kind of bright.

"You and Daddy breaking up?" I asked.

Jason stopped bouncing. It got quiet for a few seconds. Then Ma nodded. "It'll be best for everybody."

"Everybody like who?" I asked. I didn't want us to break up.

Ma said, "All of us."

"Daddy," Jason asked, "you not going to live here with us?"

"No," Daddy said.

"If it's because I'm bad all the time, I'll stop. I promise," I said. Ma was always saying I was enough to drive anybody away.

Ma tightened her arm around me. "It's nothing to do with you all," she said. "But it's very complicated."

"I understand complicated stuff," I said. "Tell me."

Daddy said, "We just need to go our separate ways."

"It's the best thing for us," Ma said.

"Where we going to live?" I asked. Some kids get put in a home.

"Here," Ma said. "This is your home. Most of all, we still love you."

"Who's going to take care of us?" Jason asked.

"Me," Ma said. "And Daddy. On weekends."

"That right, Daddy?" I asked.

"Soon as I find a nice place," he said.

"What's wrong with right here?" Jason asked.

Nobody could answer that. Daddy took out a cigarette.

4

He didn't light it. He just held it in his hand and tapped it on his thigh.

Finally Ma said, "I know it's hard to understand. It's just as hard to explain."

Jason climbed down from Daddy's lap. He came over to Ma and asked if he could go play with Julio.

"Okay," Ma said. "I'll call you when dinner's ready."

Who wanted to eat at a time like this?

When Jason was gone, Daddy said, "Come here."

I wanted to stop talking about this, but they kept on talking and making me feel worse. Daddy took my hands in his. His hands were rough and large. His knuckles must've been the size of quarters. "Don't worry. I'll be here when you need me," he said. "Try and help Jason. He's younger than you."

I hunched my shoulders. Even though I was ten and going to the fifth grade next week, I was as mixed up as Jason was. But since I was supposed to understand, I finally said, "Okay."

Daddy sighed, relieved, and said, "Good." He pulled on one of my braids. My scalp hurt when he did it. My braids were long and thick and always coming loose or getting messed up because people pull on them. I shook my braid out of Daddy's hand.

"Give me a kiss," he said. He smiled. His eyes crinkled up.

I kissed Daddy. I knew it was a good-bye kiss. I wasn't ever going to see Daddy again. I didn't care what he was promising.

2
■ ■ ■ ■ ■

Every day after I went swimming, I stopped by the auto shop. Daddy was never there. I even went sometimes before I went to the pool. Daddy still wasn't there.

On Sunday, I didn't bother to go. I went straight to the pool right after breakfast. The pool got crowded in a hurry because it was steaming hot outside. Little kids and big kids who didn't know how to swim kept bumping into me and splashing water all over my face. I was practicing swimming on my back. I kept sinking.

This one boy kicked past me twice. He splashed about ten gallons of water all over me. The water stung my eyes and shot up my nose. I coughed and coughed and crawled to the edge. I held on and shouted at him, "Watch it, creep!" But he was all the way on the other side by then and didn't hear me. The next time he was going to get it.

I let go, stretched my arms over my head and lay on top of the water. My body caved down to the bottom of the pool. I scrambled to the edge again, spat water back into the pool.

"Yuk!" someone said loud enough for me to hear.

I climbed out and saw this fat girl sitting on the red bench. She was light skinned, and her cheeks were round and red like plums. I never saw her before. I went over to her and sat down.

She made a face at me and slid over. "You put germs in the pool," she said.

I waved my hand at her. "That's why the water has chlorine. So people can spit."

"Yuk!" she said again. "Still germs."

"You don't like the water, huh?" I asked her. She had on all her clothes and I didn't see a towel or bathing suit anywhere around.

She pushed her shoulders back. "I swim. I won a medal last year."

"Oh, yeah? Then you must swim in deep water."

"Nine feet."

"Wow. It's nine feet over where the lifeguard is." I pointed to the deep side of the pool. "You dive and everything?"

She nodded. "But I don't feel like it now."

"How come? The water's real cool."

"Tomorrow."

"It closes when school starts. You have to wait till next summer."

"I can wait," she said. She took out of her pocket a small can of powder. She took off her shoes and sox and rubbed powder into her feet.

"Why you doing that?" I asked.

"Why do you think?" she asked.

"How should I know?"

"I use it so I won't get athlete's foot."

"I heard of that. Nobody around here gets that."

7

She sighed and put her sox and shoes back on. "Anybody can get it. Especially in a pool. I read it in an encyclopedia."

"You one of those bookworms?" I asked, joking with her.

She frowned and said, "No. I'm a person."

"You know what I mean. A bookworm . . ."

"I know," she said. "I read three books every week. You ever read *Huckleberry Finn*?"

"It's a Fantabulous Comic Book?"

She sighed again. "It's a novel. And it's over four hundred pages long. I didn't skip a word."

"I bet you skipped *the* and *a* plenty of times." I laughed. She didn't. "It's boring anyway."

"You never heard of it," she said. "Just like you never heard of James Baldwin."

"I have so."

"Who is he?"

I should've stayed in the water and practiced blowing bubbles. School was starting tomorrow. I'd be getting enough tests from the teacher all year. I didn't need tests from a creepy girl.

"Well?" she said.

"James is Mrs. Baldwin's son." I giggled.

She didn't giggle this time either. "What's your IQ?"

"They don't tell us in my school," I said.

Now she laughed like I'd made the biggest joke of the century. "*They* don't *tell* you your IQ. You take an IQ test."

"I hate tests," I said. And I was beginning to hate her. What kind of person talks about tests and books before school even starts?

"My mother took me to the Institute for Gifted Children. You know what my IQ is?"

"Who cares?"

"Guess," she said, poking me in the arm.

I poked her back and said, "Don't do that."

"Guess, then."

"All right. Your IQ's 10."

"Wrong. 125," she said proudly.

"Big deal. 125. I bet mine's 135."

"Not if you never heard of *Huckleberry Finn.*"

I stood up. "I'm going back in the water. See you." I wanted to dive now.

"Wait, tell me your school."

"The one down the block." I pointed to P.S. 129. It was at the other corner from the pool.

"What class?" she asked.

I walked backwards to the edge of the pool.

"Mr. Hamilton," I said. I turned around and ran.

"MR. HAMILTON! That's the smartest fifth grade. Come here."

I didn't pay any attention to her. I hoped I didn't hear what I thought I heard. I jumped in. My eyes were closed real tight. I hit the water and bumped into someone. I opened my eyes.

"You again," I said. I scooped about ten gallons of water on him to see how he liked it.

That girl was waving at me. I swam to the middle of the pool where she couldn't reach me.

3
■ ■ ■ ■

When I got out of the pool, she was still hanging around. I
tried to duck her.

"Hey, wait up." She followed me to the lockers.
"We're in the same class, you know. My name's Rhonda
Elaine Archer. What's yours?"

"Lorraine Maybe."

"That's dumb. How can your name be Lorraine
maybe?"

"No." My face was getting hot. It always did when
people made fun of me or bugged me. "My last name *is*
Maybe," I said.

She giggled. "I never heard of Maybe as a last name."

"Now you have." What she didn't know was that last
year, I knocked my clog over the head of a kid named
Victor. All year long he made fun of my name and
Crabface Crane, the fourth grade teacher, never made
him stop. So I did it myself. Only problem was, I wasn't
allowed to wear clogs anymore.

I gave the lady behind the counter the metal token and she gave me my knapsack. I looked for a room that wasn't flooded with water. I found one all the way down near the bathroom. Nobody uses this one much. It smells like pee.

Rhonda Elaine Archer followed me into the changing room.

"We're both girls," she said when I asked her to go.

"I don't like people seeing me naked, you know."

"That's baby stuff. I bet you don't have your period yet."

I grunted. I wrapped my towel around me and pulled down my bathing suit. I never thought about my period much. Ma told me about periods and babies last year. But it hasn't come yet. So I don't even think about it.

"In that case, I'll wait outside."

I stuck out my tongue at her when she closed the curtain. I got an idea how to get rid of Rhonda Elaine Archer. I took an extra long time changing my clothes.

I came out. It worked. She wasn't there. But when I got outside the locker room, she was waiting right near the door. She was fixing her white sox.

"I have to go now. My mother's waiting for me." I waved to her and walked across the street. It's wide and there used to be a lot of stores and buildings on it. Now, most of the buildings that aren't torn down are boarded up, ready to be torn down. Rusty cans, sticks, bricks, old refrigerators, glass, furniture and clothes are thrown all over the vacant lots. It's like a big garbage can. Everybody uses it.

"I live down this block, too," she said.

I crossed my fingers and asked, "Which building do you live in?" Even though I never saw her before today, she

11

could've moved into my building in the middle of the night. Some people do that when they sneak out of their old building for not paying their rent. They sneak into the new building and act like they've always lived there.

"2180," she said.

"Oh. I'm 2184. There used to be another building between ours. They tore it down last year." All over the Bronx buildings were being torn down.

"How come?"

"Rats."

She screamed. "Rats!"

Who wasn't scared of rats? They're terrible. "I heard about a kid. He got eaten by one. It was on the news. Now my mother won't let me eat in bed," I said. Her face was all twisted up. "You see, they, uh, smell the crumbs on your face. That's why they eat you." I pinched her arm to make like nibbling.

She jerked away. "Stop. You're not scared?"

"No."

"If you're not, I'm not either."

"You are too."

"Am not."

"Wait'll you see one," I said. "We'll see who's scared then."

"What makes you think I'll see one?"

"Because, they live in the walls. Wait awhile. You'll hear them."

I walked into the vacant lot on the corner before we got to Rhonda's building. I found a long stick. Nails were sticking out of it, so I had to be careful. I used the stick to pick through the garbage. "A man once found a thousand-dollar bill in a vacant lot."

12

"You saw him?"

"No, a boy named Warren told me." I pushed away a bunch of trash. The perfect place for a thousand-dollar bill to be hiding. There was nothing but some pieces of grass starting to grow. "Need a new jacket?" I asked laughing. I held up a raggedy black jacket on the end of the stick. It had only one sleeve.

"Very funny." Rhonda marched out of the lot. Her head was stuck high in the air.

I came out, too. I never did find anything valuable.

"Did you move away in the middle of the night?"

"No." She was insulted. She must know about middle of the night movers. "It was eleven o'clock."

"Close enough." I laughed.

"Plenty of people move out at night."

"I know they do." I took a piece of gum out of my pocket.

"Give me some," she said before I even unwrapped the gum.

I broke it in two, measured it, and gave her the smaller piece.

"Boy, you're stingy," she said, looking at her tiny piece of gum. She rolled it up, then put it in her mouth and chewed like a cow.

"Beggars can't be choosy," I said.

4

"Ma!" I called, and slammed the front door so hard the walls shook. It was close to dinnertime, and so Ma was in the kitchen cooking. Except at mealtimes she was either studying or drawing. Ma was going to college to be a fashion designer. "Ma," I said, coming into the kitchen. "I just met the stinkiest girl in the world. She swears she's the smartest person alive."

Ma stirred the big orange pot. The steam was streaming up to the ceiling. I peeked in the pot. Beef stew.

"Can I buy pizza, please?"

"Wash up. Dinner'll be ready soon," she said.

"Ma, her name is Rhonda Elaine Archer." I imitated Rhonda's proper voice. "You ever heard of James Baldwin?" I asked, sure she hadn't.

"Who hasn't?"

"What did he do that's so great anyway?"

"He's a world-famous writer."

"Is that all?" I asked, and took a banana out of the fruit

bowl. I stood on a chair and went through the cabinet. I pulled out a can of sardines and got down.

"Put that away. I told you dinner'll be ready soon."

"I'm hungry. Swimming always does that to me."

Ma always claimed I was too skinny and too short for my age. Sometimes she said I must have a tapeworm that ate all the food I put into my mouth. No matter how much I ate, I stayed skinny.

"But don't put bananas on the sandwich."

"I like it that way."

"You'll get sick."

"No, I won't." I sliced the banana and put it on the side of the bread with the mayonnaise.

"What did I tell you?" Ma yelled, her hands on her hips.

"What's the difference, eating them together or eating the banana last?"

"Plenty. Now, do like I tell you."

"Okay. I'm going to eat in the living room," I said, putting my sandwich and banana on a plate together.

"No. Crumbs'll get all down in the couch. Sit at the table and eat."

Ma turned around and stirred in some other pots on the stove. Very quietly I put some banana slices on my sandwich and closed it before Ma turned back around.

Ma got out the cornmeal, eggs, milk, butter. "Oooo, let me make the cornbread," I said, and jumped up. My hand brushed against the plate. The plate crashed on the floor.

"What am I going to do with you?" Ma wiped her hands on the tail of the old shirt she was wearing. It used to belong to Daddy. But Ma wore it whenever she cooked or sewed. She said it was comfortable. It reminded me of Daddy and when we were a family, and when he was coming home for dinner.

Ma bent down and helped me pick up the broken pieces. "Careful," she said. She was angry at me. "All I need now is for you to cut yourself. Jesus," Ma said almost to herself. "What am I going to do?"

Ma got the mop and pail. She mopped the entire kitchen floor. I stood at the refrigerator watching her push the mop back and forth and wiping off sweat.

"Want me to help?" I asked.

"No. Just go play." She waved me away.

Ma didn't want to be bothered with me. So I went into my bedroom. It was the same as the living room. Our house only had three rooms. Jason and I slept on two pullout couches in the living room. His was on one side of the room; mine was on the other.

I went through my knapsack, looking for my jacks. I only found six. One of them was smashed. Then I couldn't find the ball. A hole was at the bottom, and maybe the ball went through it with the other four jacks. I felt like crying for no reason. But I didn't. I turned on the television. The picture was all fuzzy. The antennas needed fixing. Daddy said he was going to do it. He never got the chance to do it. This time, I did cry into the sofa cushion.

5

■ ■ ■ ■ ■

Rhonda bounced down the steps to her building. "Hi, Lorraine," she called and waved. The plaid dress she was wearing flopped as she moved. She looked like a chubby ballerina. Her hair was curled under in the back. Her bangs were curled up like a fat sausage. The rest of her hair was okay.

"That's a pretty hairdo," I said, wondering if Ma'd ever let me wear my hair in curls. Not the bangs part, though.

"Thanks." She pulled up her white sox.

She didn't even look at the new pantsuit I was wearing. "At least you can say something nice about me."

"You look nice too." She started walking fast because it was almost time for the school bell to ring. "We're going to be late," she said. "And it's just the first day."

"So." I spat on the sidewalk. "I hope a grown-up trips and falls in my spit."

"Yuk! You're so nasty." Rhonda made a face. I stuck my tongue out at her. She was a goody-goody. I could see that already.

17

The DON'T WALK sign started to flash off and on. Rhonda stopped at the curb. I shot across the street. A brown car with a beige top put on its brakes real hard. The driver yelled at me. "You want to get killed?"

"Shove it," I yelled back at her.

When Rhonda finally got to the other side of the street, she said, "Oooo! I heard you all the way over on the other side."

"People make me mad."

"Me, too," Rhonda said, but she didn't say who made her mad. I didn't tell her who made me mad. We just went to find our class.

All the classes were lined up in the yard. The teachers held up big blue, pink, yellow or red signs. The blue signs were for the fifth grade. We went to where all the blues were, then looked for 5–440.

"That's our class," I said.

It was a man teacher holding the sign up. He must've been ten feet tall. He had a red beard and big red Afro.

"I think I want to go back home," I said, stopping as we got closer to our class.

"You can't go home on the first day," Rhonda said. Rhonda kept saying "Excuse me, excuse me," as she pushed her way through all the kids. She went right away to her size place in line.

If I went to my size place, I'd be first in line. I slipped in between a girl with long, curly black hair and Millie, who was in my class last year.

"Hey, Lorraine," Warren said. He was in line right next to me. He must've grown three inches over the summer. He still wore his glasses with the thick lenses and carried that funny-looking bookbag with the little leather straps. Most kids were carrying green knapsacks across their backs.

"Hi, Warren." I looked away. Warren used to be my partner on line in third grade. Now he was way taller than me.

"He's waiting for you to get in your size place," Warren whispered.

I peeked up at the teacher. His hands were folded behind his back. He was staring right at me, but not saying anything. The kids looked at me too. Millie poked me in the back.

"Young lady, we're waiting for you," he said softly.

"Me?" I poked myself in the chest.

He didn't answer me. All the other classes were going up to their rooms. We were the only class left in the yard.

"Come on, Lorraine," Millie whispered.

"Get in line," someone else said.

"Mind your business," I said, and walked to the front of the line.

The teacher nodded. The first boy started walking. So I started walking, leading the girls' line into the school.

Nobody said a word all the way up to the class, not even me.

When we got to the room, he said, "You can sit where you want."

"Well, all right," I said, sitting next to Rhonda.

"Shush," Rhonda said.

"Boy, he's easy," I whispered to Rhonda.

She waved her hand at me, then folded her hands across her desk. She stared at the teacher.

I nudged her. "You hear me? I never had an easy teacher before."

19

"Shut up," Rhonda said. She didn't even move her lips.

The teacher walked in front of my desk and stood there. He told us his name, which was Weston Hamilton. He liked to ski, read books, and travel. He was the first teacher I knew who ever did anything besides give a lot of homework and tests. He even told us he'd been teaching for a year.

I whispered to Rhonda again, "I bet he's been teaching fifty years. Don't you think?"

Rhonda took out a piece of paper, not from her loose-leaf notebook, but from a little pad. She wrote me a note and put it on my lap.

Rhonda raised her hand and the teacher looked over as I was about to read it. Rhonda asked, "Is this 5–1?"

The teacher cleared his throat. "We don't have 5–1, 5–2 in this school."

"But, I'm supposed to be in the smartest class." Then she told the class about the institute she was tested at. Nobody thought it was a big deal. Not even the teacher, I don't think.

He said, "It's better this way."

"You mean," Rhonda said, waving her finger across the room, "everybody's mixed in. Even the dumb kids?"

"Who she think she is?"

"What makes her so smart?" There were more grunts and moans.

The teacher held up his hand for us to be quiet. Since it was the first day and all, we got quiet pretty quick. "There's no such thing as a dumb kid," he said. "Everybody is good at something." Rhonda was shaking her head. "Think on it," he said.

I guess Rhonda was thinking about it. She was pretty

quiet for awhile. The teacher told us to write about what we did over the summer. Everyone got busy writing. The summer was something I wanted to forget, not put down on paper for the teacher and anybody else to read.

So I didn't do it.

I unfolded Rhonda's note. It said, "You think you're funny. You're not. If you want to get in trouble, that's your problem. But I don't want to get in trouble with you. So leave me alone."

I crushed it up and threw it on the floor underneath Rhonda's desk. I drew little circles and curly things in the margin of my paper and waited for the teacher to do something interesting.

6

This was a boring class. All morning we took a bunch of tests. None of them was an IQ test, I don't think. So I couldn't prove to Rhonda that my IQ was higher than hers. I couldn't even tell her what the letters *i* and *q* stood for. I hope she never asks.

After lunch, Mr. Hamilton started to pry information out of us.

"Can I go to the bathroom?" I asked, shifting around in my seat.

"Later." He asked Nereida about herself.

"I went to Puerto Rico this summer. Me and my cousins climbed a mountain. You ever been to P.R.?"

He shook his head.

"Brother," I said.

"Lorraine Maybe . . ." His voice was deep like a tuba. If he yelled, he'd probably break all the windows. But he didn't yell at me.

The class roared. One boy said, pointing at me, "Her name's Maybe."

"Want one of these?" I called, showing him my fist.

Mr. Hamilton reached over and lowered my fist to my desk. "Don't touch me." I jerked away.

He gave a long speech about respecting each other and listening to each other. When he finished, I said, "Now can I go to the bathroom?"

"You haven't heard a word I've said." I hunched my shoulders. "Politeness is one of the class rules."

"Dag, I didn't make the stupid rules."

All of a sudden the room got real quiet. All my insides felt like they were crunching up together. The teacher stood up slowly. He stared down at me with his big, brown eyes. He rubbed his hairy arms as he walked back and forth across the front of the room. He scratched his beard. It gave me the chills.

He sat back down. "Lorraine, tell the class about yourself."

That's a relief! Miss Crane would've sent me to the assistant principal, plus sent a letter home. He's not going to. I bet he'd let you get away with anything.

I sucked my teeth. "Everybody knows me. You know me too. I bet you read my record card already."

"Tell us anyway." He sat on the edge of Nereida's desk. Nereida covered her mouth and giggled. She glanced at Millie, and Millie giggled too. They must've thought he was cute. I didn't. He looked kind of ridiculous to me. When he sat down, his pants leg rose up. Hair was sticking out from over his sock. Boy, were his legs ugly. So was his face, all covered with freckles. He was the first black person I'd ever seen with freckles. Rhonda had the same complexion he did, but she didn't have freckles. "Go on," he said.

"Well, this is eass—see!" I counted each thing off on

23

my fingers. "I like five things about school. Number one—recess." The class laughed. "Number two—lunch. Three—when the teacher is absent. Three o'clock. Free time. Trips."

The class roared. Some stupid boy fell out of his chair laughing.

Mr. Hamilton laughed too. His laugh was more like a pig snorting. All that hair, freckles and the snorting. I bet after three o'clock he changes into a creepy half-animal, half-man thing. He might even be a wolfman because that's exactly what he reminded me of.

I started to laugh, but nobody knew the real reason.

"You should stop," Rhonda said. She rolled her eyes at me. I felt like punching her in one of her plum cheeks.

"Trips makes six things," Wolfman said. That name fit him.

"You can't count either," Rhonda whispered to me. She was lucky I ignored her this time.

"Speaking of trips," Wolfman said, "I've planned a lot for this year."

I didn't care. I wouldn't be going on any.

"The Botanical Garden, the Zoo, Planetarium. The Metropolitan Museum of Art."

I moaned out loud.

Rhonda called out. "Mr. Hamilton, when can we get new seats?"

7

It was after seven o'clock when Ma got home. Tonight she had school, plus she worked at Macy's. I fixed some sandwiches for Jason and me because Ma would be too tired to cook when she got home.

As soon as Jason heard Ma's keys jingle in the door, he rushed to the door and pulled it open.

"Jason, you're not supposed to open the door," I screamed at him.

"It's Ma," he said. "I knew it." He hugged Ma real tight. She looked too tired to give him a real good hug back. She patted his head.

"You been good?" she asked, and dragged herself inside. She threw her pocketbook and the portfolio she kept her design sketches in on the couch.

"Lorraine wouldn't let me go outside."

"I told her not to."

I licked my tongue at Jason. "Are we going to see Daddy this weekend?"

"Not to my knowledge," Ma said.

"How come?" Jason asked. "I miss him."

"Your father's a very busy man." Ma was sticking up for him.

"That's not the reason," I said.

"No? What, then?"

"He hates me."

Ma looked surprised. Since Daddy left, we hadn't talked about him. Ma never even told us why they broke up. But the last thing Daddy did say was, "I'll be back for you. Wait and see."

It's been a month. I'm still waiting.

8
■ ■ ■ ■ ■

The first week of October, Wolfman gave us new seats. My seat was in the front near his desk. He called Rhonda's name for the seat next to mine.

I stood up. "Let me sit in the back."

"No," Wolfman said. "Michael, sit here. Leroy, here. Warren"—he pointed to a desk two rows over. Michael, Leroy, and Warren took their seats without a word.

"How come? You said these seats were temporary." I tapped my foot.

"This is your seat." He put his finger on my loose leaf. I snatched it up. Most of the time, teachers like me to sit in the back. What's wrong with him?

"Do you intend to sit down?" he asked.

I rolled my eyes. "Let me sit back there. I can't see the board when I sit this close."

"Mr. Hamilton, let her sit back there," Rhonda said.

Wolfman ignored Rhonda. He said to me, "We won't be using the board that much. Now . . . sit."

"Can I change my seat later?"

"Sit."

"Let me go to the bathroom first." I twisted one leg behind the other.

"No."

"Sit down, Lorraine," Rhonda said. "You're wasting our time."

"Since when you're the boss of the class?"

"I'm the president of the class."

"So. I didn't vote for you. I voted for Nereida."

"All right. Lorraine and Rhonda, stop it."

"Make her sit down, teacher," Leroy called out. Leroy wore a black leather glove on one hand. He banged that hand on his desk. He had a nerve to talk. He used to always be sitting in the office for shooting spitballs during math.

Wolfman walked up the aisle, giving out the rest of the seats. He said, "Lorraine doesn't have to sit down. She can stand all morning if she wants to."

The class roared.

I slowly slid into my seat. It was a long time till lunch.

When it was time for lunch, ours was the last class to eat because Wolfman took forever bringing us down the stairs. I asked Nereida where she got her shoes and he made the class go back upstairs and start all over again.

The kids were mad and grumbling because we were so far back on line. I laughed and laughed. I had brought my lunch, and I sat down at the table to eat.

"Come with me," Wolfman said.

"Who? Me? I just sat down."

He stood over me waiting for me to get up. I started to undo the foil on my sandwich.

"It wasn't only me," I said, and shoved the sandwich back into the brown paper bag. I went back to the room with him.

He sat at his desk. He opened his *New York Times* to the crossword puzzle. He dug into his lunch like this was the first meal he'd had in days.

The windows were wide open. The kids in the yard were yelling, running, and playing while I was stuck in this room all period.

"Better not keep me in tomorrow. I'll run out. And you can't stop me."

He chomped on his hero. A slice of tomato slid out. He picked it up and ate it. Slob, I thought. I didn't have the nerve to say that out loud.

"Those are the wrong answers you're filling in. Ha. Ha."

He handed me the newspaper. "Want to try?"

I shook my head. My braids flopped from side to side. One braid had come loose since this morning. I braided it back up.

"Here," he said, still shoving the paper at me.

"Thanks, but no thanks. I got better things to do."

I opened my notebook to a clean page and drew Donald Duck, Spiderman, and a wolfman. "Can I use the crayons?"

"No, sit down."

"You blind or something? I *am* sitting."

He glanced up from his paper. When he stuck his head back, he smiled. "So you are."

Big deal, I'm staying in my seat like he told me. He's not making me sit down. It's just that I really did find something better to do.

29

When I started to draw Spiderman crawling up the wall, I stopped hearing the noises from the yard. Except for when I was drawing Wolfman, I forgot he was even in the room with me.

Since I wasn't allowed to get the crayons, I pressed sometimes hard and sometimes soft on my pencil to make different shades. At the end, I put a dimple in Wolfman's right cheek. He didn't really have a dimple there, I don't think. But it seemed he should. I had one on each cheek.

"Lorraine." He was shaking my shoulder. "Come on."

I covered my drawings real quick. He might get mad if he saw himself. He might even laugh at me.

"Lunch is over. Didn't you hear the bell?"

"Uh-uh." I stuffed my papers in the pocket of my notebook. "It's like we're in a forest and we can't hear any bells. This is fun."

He walked toward the door. He held it open for me. No teacher ever did that for me. "Staying in is meant to teach you a lesson."

"Well—learning this lesson is fun." I grinned.

He laughed. He did have a dimple, a long skinny one.

I used to stay in a lot. But this staying in was better than playing hopscotch, jumping rope, and playing jacks. It was a hundred times better than staying home waiting for Jason to come home from day care and for Ma to come home from work.

9

"Daddy!" Jason shouted, jumping up from watching the TV, which he sits two inches from because the picture is all fuzzy.

Daddy was wearing a new brown hat and coat to match. He was growing a moustache. He looked different.

I threw down the paper I was drawing on. I ran to him. "About time."

He bent over for me to kiss him. Then he picked up Jason. Jason hugged him and laid his face up against Daddy's.

"Well," Ma said. "Why didn't you tell me you were coming?" She seemed nervous. She tucked the tail of her shirt in her pants, then patted her hair down.

"Been busy. You know, I don't work at the shop anymore."

Ma shook her head. "No. I didn't know that."

Daddy put Jason down. Jason tried to pull Daddy into the kitchen. "Want some dinner?" Jason asked.

Daddy looked at Ma. Ma stared back at him. She shrugged. "It's okay."

I cleaned Ma's books and papers off the table to make room for Daddy to eat.

Daddy looked over one of Ma's books. He laid it back in my arms. Ma set a plate in front of him. Digging into the pot roast and mashed potatoes, he said, "You're still the best cook out of South Carolina." That's what he always said to Ma. When he didn't like what she cooked, he blamed it on her designing and on college. But tonight, he only had nice things to say. When he looked at Ma cleaning up the kitchen, he had a sparkle in his eyes. I bet they still loved each other.

Ma wiped off the stove. Afterwards, she said, "You came to see the kids. I'll be in the other room."

"You don't have to go," I said. "Does she, Daddy?"

Daddy looked at Ma with that sparkly look. "Stay, Aggie. What I have to tell you all is something else."

"What, Daddy, what?" Jason asked, bouncing on Daddy's leg as if it were a trampoline.

"Remember the shop I was telling you all about?"

"Yeah." For as long as I could remember, Daddy's been saying that he was going to buy his own auto repair shop. He'd be his own boss, make his own hours, and tell everyone else what to do.

"I bought it."

"Wow. When can we go see it?" I asked.

"I want to go now," Jason whined.

Daddy gave Jason a little sock in the jaw. Jason gave Daddy one back. "Soon, soon."

"Where's the shop, James?" Ma asked. She wasn't as excited as we were.

"On Southern Boulevard?" I asked. That was the best place for his shop to be. A lot of cars break down on Southern Boulevard. Besides, Southern Boulevard is not far from here.

"It's in Queens."

"Queens!"

"Stop yelling," Daddy said.

"But Queens is far from here."

"Not that far. You'll see when you come spend the weekend."

"You live there too?" Jason asked.

"The most important reason for moving is so you and Jason'll have a nice place to stay when you come out."

Daddy jiggled my braid and poked me in the side, trying to make me smile. His poking was tickling me. So I finally smiled. I wasn't smiling inside.

"You'll love it. There're trees up and down the block. There's a big yard in back of the building for all the kids."

"You coming too, Ma?" Jason asked. "We all going to live in Queens?"

"I wish I had some tape for your big mouth," I said.

"Lorraine, please," Ma said.

I leaned against Ma. She put her arm around me.

"You, your mother and Lorraine'll live here. But you'll come and visit me."

"Do I have to sleep in the living room?" I asked. "I want my own room for a change."

"No. There's a room for both of you. Wait till you see it."

I leaned up from Ma. "My own room?" I asked, not believing my ears. "What time on Friday you picking us up?"

"Uh, I'm not, not this week."

Ma slammed her hand down on the table. "Why did you get them all excited now?"

"It's okay, Ma." I said. They didn't hear me. They started arguing like they used to.

"Stay out of this, Aggie." Daddy set Jason on the floor.

"I won't. You're being unfair and selfish. Don't you think they have feelings? They're looking forward to seeing you and being with you. And you're just getting their hopes up for a letdown."

Daddy faced me and Jason. "Don't worry. As soon as the apartment is fixed up, I'll come for you. I just signed the lease yesterday." He laughed and said, "My own children can't sleep on the floor."

"I like sleeping on the floor," Jason said.

"It's true," I said. "In the mornings, he's always wrapped up in his covers on the floor." I pulled on Daddy's arm. "Let us come Friday."

"Stop, Lorraine." Daddy brushed my hand away. "I already told you, not this weekend."

Ma shook her head and said, "Look, it's past their bedtime."

"No, it's not. 'Hawaii Five–O' didn't come on yet," Jason said.

"I'm getting nice beds for both of you. You'll like it." He picked up Jason and kissed him. Then he put his cheek to my face for me to kiss him. "Behaving yourself in school?" He asked like he already knew the answer was no.

"The teacher makes her stay in," Jason blurted out.

"Be quiet, Jason," Ma said. "And go wash up for bed."

Daddy squinted up his eyes. Daddy didn't beat me or

yell at me. He closed his eyes until they were two narrow slits, fluttering with anger and disappointment. Daddy always used to say he was angry at me or disappointed in me. "We had enough of you being bad to last a lifetime. I want to see straight A's this year." He shook his finger at me.

"Yes, sir," I said. Suddenly I wished Daddy would go. After all this time waiting for him to come back, I wished he'd go. And I also wished he could be proud of me.

Ma put her arms around me and said, "She's doing much better this year. She likes school *and* her teacher."

Ma gave me a little squeeze and smile. I knew it meant for me to keep my mouth shut. I was kind of mixed-up. When Daddy was here and everything was fine, Ma sided with him. She was always saying, "Lorraine, you can do better. Put your mind to it." Or, "Lorraine, do this. Don't do that." And, "This homework paper is a mess."

Now, Ma squeezed me. The slits in Daddy's eyes opened a little bit. He nodded like he was saying to himself, "All right. We'll see."

He pulled his fur collar up around his neck and said, "About time."

Before Daddy went out the door, Jason ran back in to get another kiss from Daddy. He hadn't been washing, because chocolate pudding was still stuck to his face. He was soaking wet. Jason had been playing in the water again, trying to make the Ivory soap sink. He always plays instead of washing, and I bet he is the dirtiest kid on the block. Daddy didn't care. He gave Jason a big, wet kiss right where the crusty hard pudding was.

"Don't go," Jason whined. He locked his arms around Daddy's neck. Daddy tried to unlock his arms.

"I have to go, partner," Daddy said, tugging at Jason's arms. Jason's legs dangled in the air.

"Jason," Ma said calmly, "Daddy has to go." She eased Jason's arms loose.

Jason said, "No. No." He started kicking wildly.

Ma lifted Jason away from Daddy and set him on the floor. "You know better," she said.

"That's no way for a big boy to act," Daddy said, embarrassed because he couldn't get Jason loose and Ma could do it with only a few words. "I'm coming back," he said.

"He'll be okay." Ma started to take the cushions off the couch, and told me to take Jason and make sure he washed.

"Then—I'll call," Daddy said. "Next week."

Ma nodded.

Jason said, "Promise?"

"Promise," Daddy said. Daddy left us again.

10

Everybody ran from the lunch line to the tables to get the seats they wanted. I saw Rhonda coming. I slid right into the end seat. Nereida and Claribel slid into the end seats across the table. We had to sit close together because after lunch we were playing a double Dutch tournament. Rhonda didn't know how to jump. She wasn't in the tournament.

Rhonda put her tray down next to mine. "I sit here."

I opened my lunch and said, "First come, first served."

"You make me sick," she said.

Nereida and Claribel giggled. Rhonda frowned and squeezed into the tiny space I'd left. I elbowed her. She elbowed me back.

"Somebody smells fishy," Rhonda sang so everyone could hear.

"Who? Me?" Leroy asked. Leroy was sitting next to Warren on the other side of Claribel.

"I don't smell like fish," Millie said.

"Me neither," Warren said.

"It's my sardines," I said. My voice was low so only Rhonda could hear.

"Yuk!" she said, holding her nose. "They must be contaminated."

I flapped my hand at her and started eating. Rhonda had two lunches. The school lunch and the lunch she brought from home. Brown bread with beige speckles in it. A thick hunk of white cheese and long, snakey white strings hanging out.

"Now, that's contamination if you ask me," I said to Nereida.

"Right." Nereida giggled. Her giggles bubbled out like water boiling. Even when you didn't know what was funny, you had to laugh along with Nereida.

Rhonda rolled her eyes at us. She always did when we made fun of the lunches she brought from home. Once she brought little tomatoes, celery and carrot sticks and lettuce leaves. "Pet food," we called it. It didn't matter to Rhonda. She ate what she brought from home, plus the school lunch. And she was supposed to be on a diet.

Rhonda stuck her sandwich in my face. "This is fresh food. Those sardines came in a can."

"Like I didn't know," I said.

Nereida nodded.

"And cans can give you botulism." Rhonda stirred her chocolate powder in the container of milk.

Leroy banged his fist on the table. He didn't know what Rhonda was talking about either. But he pretended it was funny.

"Botu—— who?" I asked, curious about what Miss Know-it-all meant now.

"I never heard of it," Leroy said with a wave of his hand.

38

Rhonda said, "That's nothing. You never heard of three times six either."

Nobody laughed except Rhonda. We didn't make fun of Leroy. He never did any work. I don't think he knew too much either.

"Botulism is when germs . . . it's when germs get inside the can. You die from it."

"That's a lie," I said.

Rhonda shrugged. "Don't believe me." She finished the meatballs and started on her lunch from home. "Here. You can have some of my sandwich."

Those snakes dangling out made me gag. "No, thanks," I said. I prayed I wasn't getting that botu-whatever-it-was because those sardines were dee—licious. I ate my lunch.

A little while later, Rhonda whispered in my ear. "I just heard Nereida talk about you."

"My lunch," I said. "Everybody does."

Rhonda shook her head. "Uh-uh. She was talking in Spanish. I heard her."

"So what? She's Spanish," I said.

"But I know Spanish," Rhonda said. "She said *padre. Padre* is *father.* They were talking about *your* father."

"My father!" I yelled, and jumped up. "You better watch it," I said to Nereida.

"Huh?" Nereida acted like she was innocent.

"I don't like people talking about my father."

Claribel sucked her teeth. "Who's talking—"

"Mind your business," I said.

"But I wasn't," Nereida said, and she climbed out of her seat.

"Uh-huh. Yeah. Sure." I was going to get her. I looked around for something.

Rhonda got up to dump her tray.

39

I grabbed a handful of rice off it, put it in my mouth, and shot the rice through a straw. Rice stuck all over Nereida's hair and eyebrows and face.

Nereida punched me in the arm. I punched her back.

"Fight. Fight," kids yelled. Kids from other tables ran over. They jumped on the tables to watch.

Somebody pulled us apart. Then a man grabbed me and pinned my arms behind my back. It hurt. I couldn't get loose. Nereida kicked me.

"You let her kick me on purpose," I screamed.

He carried me out of the lunchroom. I kicked and kicked, aiming at his knee. "Get off of me. Get off of me."

Just then Wolfman came tearing out of the teacher's lunchroom. He acted like a wild man. "Put her down," he said.

"She's going crazy," the man said. "Look at her."

"Get off of me!" I kicked as hard as I could. I hit some bone.

"Oooow!" The man let go of me.

Wolfman said, "I'm her teacher. I'll take over."

"This kid should be locked up," the man said.

"You don't even know how it started," I yelled at him.

Teachers were standing in the hall watching and shaking their heads. Crabby Crane, my last year's teacher, was there. I heard her say to another teacher, "Hasn't changed." They went back inside.

Wolfman said, "Come with me." He started down the hall.

"Don't touch me." My mouth filled up with tears. They were burning my face. I couldn't stop shaking.

"Nobody's hurting you now," he said. He put his arm around me and led me into a tiny room at the far end of the hall. We sat at a small round table facing each other.

He let me cry until I was finished and just sniffling. He gave me a tobacco-smelling handkerchief so I could blow my nose. I hate tobacco smells. I held the handkerchief, but I wouldn't use it.

"Blow your nose," Wolfman said. He put his hand over mine. I jerked away.

"Why don't you yell and get it over with? For your information, it wasn't all my fault."

"Tell me."

I told him the whole story, starting with how Rhonda barged her way into the seat at the table. "Then that man grabbed me and dug his nails into my arm. I'm going to make my father sue him."

Wolfman smiled. "I'll speak to him."

"He must hate kids." I rubbed my arm where it was sore.

"Getting back to our problem," Wolfman said. "It looks like you're taking words too seriously. Words can't hurt."

I nodded my head up and down. "Oh, yes." A lot he didn't know about words. It was words when Daddy said he was leaving. It was words when he said I am a disappointment.

"Besides, what right do you have to shoot rice at Nereida?"

"You're just like all teachers, siding with Nereida because she's quiet and does her homework and gets hundreds on spelling tests."

"What gives you the right?" he asked again.

"This." I shook my fist at him. "Nobody talks about my father and gets away with it."

"How do you know she did?"

41

"I know."

"Did you hear her?" I didn't answer him. "Think on it."

The end-of-lunch buzzer sounded. Wolfman kept talking.

"You love your father. But you can't . . ."

I jumped up. "Are you going to suspend me?"

In this school, you get suspended for fighting. Your parents have to come to school for them to let you back in.

Wolfman sighed, "I'll do what needs to be done."

Tears filled my eyes. I was shaking all over. "I hate you. I hate this school."

I ran out of the room and down the hall. I pushed and shoved my way past kids coming in from the yard.

I wasn't ever going back into that school. Not in a million years.

11

I ran up the block to where the pool is. I sat on the stone ledge, out of breath and hot. Then suddenly blasts of cold air stung my cheeks like a thousand needles. I started to freeze. But I couldn't go back to school. They might suspend me. Daddy would never come back to see me or take me to his house. Or Ma might get fed up and put me in a home.

I hopped on one foot, then the other. That didn't help. I was still cold. I turned my pockets inside out. All my money was in school in my knapsack. But I couldn't go back. In the back pocket of my blue jeans I found a dime. I ran across the street to the candy store.

The candy store was narrow, dingy, and empty. The man inside was the owner. His head was half-gray and half-bald. He looked to be about two thousand years old. He was emptying boxes of cookies into glass jars. I picked through the tray of two-cent candy and bought mints and bubble gum.

He didn't allow you to eat in the store or stay inside if you weren't buying anything. So I ate my mints at the magazine rack. I pretended I was looking for a special magazine. I spinned the rickety rack round and round.

"What you looking for?" the owner called out. He hobbled over and took a magazine out of my hand.

"Uh . . ." All I thought of were the magazines Ma bought, *Vogue* and *Harper's Bazaar*.

"Don't carry them." He put the magazine back on the rack any old where.

"What about *Essence*? That's a black one."

"That neither." He squinted his eyes at me, then looked at his clock. "Don't you belong in school? It's past one."

It was only ten after. I had two hours to kill.

"It's a half-day." I went to the pinball machines. Sometimes you get a free shot. Even if you can't, the lights go on when you pull the plunger.

He put his hand over the plunger. "Don't like hooky players hanging around my store." He shooed me away like a fly.

"I'm not a hooky player." I walked backwards to the door. "Since when can't you look around a store?"

He slammed the glass door in my face. I was out in the cold again. Two hours before I could go home. There were some good TV shows on now. I had the key. But it was in my knapsack. Everything was in my knapsack. Jacks. Jump rope. Money. Cookies. Magic Markers.

I crossed back to the school side of the street. I ran to keep warm. The school buzzer went off. It sounded like a long, sloppy burp. It was the end of sixth period and time for social studies. But not for me. I hate social studies anyway.

44

Today, though, the groups were starting. Each group was doing a different region of the United States. My group was the New England states. I was the leader. Wolfman picked me. Would he suspend someone who was a leader? No. But I bet he'd suspend someone who was a leader and who was playing hooky.

I wasn't playing hooky. Not on purpose anyway. I could go back now and just be late. Being late wasn't as bad as playing hooky. Wolfman didn't say for sure he was going to suspend me. I had to go back and find out what he was going to do. Besides, I needed my knapsack.

I walked into the main office. "Let me have a late pass," I said to Mrs. Barretto. She was the secretary.

She got up from the typewriter. She took a late pass out of the box that was on top of the file cabinet. She didn't need to ask me my name and class.

"Thanks," I said, and headed for the room. Nobody stopped me in the hall. That meant nobody was looking for me. No alarms were out.

All the kids were sitting in their small groups. Everybody was talking all at once, and no one noticed me come in. Wolfman was working with Millie's group. I was glad he didn't see me, because I didn't know how to explain about running away.

I went to my group. Nereida and Rhonda and Warren were in the same group as me. Warren was writing in the brown notebook. The rule was that only the leaders were allowed to write in those brown books.

"That's mine," I said, reaching for the book.

Rhonda put her arm out, blocking me from Warren. Warren sat still.

"What are you doing?" I asked.

45

Warren didn't speak up until Rhonda poked him in the side. Then he said, "I'm . . . *I'm* the leader now."

"We voted you out," Rhonda said. "It was unanimous."

"Unanimous? You can't . . ." I couldn't finish the sentence. Nobody was siding with me. Not Nereida. Not Warren.

But, since when can people vote you out of something like this? Only Wolfman could change the leaders.

"I'm doing land and resources," Rhonda told Warren. I sat down hard. Warren just sat, looking at the book. Rhonda grabbed it from him. "What about you, Nereida?"

Nereida's elbows dug into her knees and her hands held her head. She looked disgusted. I was too.

"We got to finish this. Mr. Hamilton's coming to us soon," Rhonda said. "You do climate, Nereida."

Nereida sat up. "No. That's not the one I was supposed . . ."

Michael shook his head. "I want to do climate."

"Nereida's doing it," Rhonda said. "You do agriculture." She pointed to me and said, "You do cities."

"No," I said. "We're doing this all wrong."

"And I want to do cities," Nereida said. "You tricked us, Rhonda, into voting for Warren."

Rhonda pressed her lips together. She waggled her hand at Nereida and wrote down what she wanted everybody to do. Nothing we said made any difference.

Nereida mumbled, "This is the worst group."

"You said it," I said. Suddenly I hated Rhonda. Warren would never have taken my place as leader. Come to think of it, Nereida would never say or do anything mean or nasty. Rhonda was the one who did stuff like that.

Wolfman came over at last. He took the book from Rhonda and nodded his head. "All done? And so fast? That's good."

"See," Rhonda said, smiling.

"You know why?" I said. Then I told him the whole story of how Rhonda bossed everybody around and wanted things her way.

He gave me a look. "Of course, Rhonda can't be leader," he said. "Not this way."

I clapped.

He went on. "But frankly, Lorraine, you're not responsible enough."

"I am responsible. Really. Give me another chance. You'll see. Please."

Rhonda shook her head. "Some people! Won't catch me begging."

"Why don't you shut up," Warren said.

I didn't care if I was begging. Being the group leader was the best thing that ever happened to me in school up to now. I wasn't going to let Rhonda get away with tricking me out of it, plus making me enemies with Nereida.

"I'll be responsible from now on," I promised. "And I'm sorry about *everything*."

Wolfman scratched his beard. He was thinking it over. He stared me straight in the eyes like he was putting a spell on me. He spoke real slow. I didn't miss one single word. "One last chance," he said. "And that's it."

12

Two weeks later the groups ended. Our group got the second highest score. The Southwest got the highest. I was sorry when it was over because it was a lot of fun.

Then two good things happened. I apologized to Nereida, and I wasn't suspended for fighting. Also, Wolfman stopped keeping me in after school. But it was so lonely at home, I ended up staying in anyway, helping him or drawing.

I sat at my desk drawing while he marked papers. He smiled at me and said, "Why don't you go home? You should start your homework. You have plenty to catch up on."

"There's the whole entire weekend. I got nothing to do."

"Nothing?" He looked surprised.

I didn't want to go into it, about Daddy in Queens and the visit we never had. I just said, "It all depends."

He started to mark Wednesday's science homework. I

had to make up that too. "Who got a hundred?" I asked.

He didn't answer. He was so involved in the papers. That happened sometimes.

"Don't you have things to do at home? Mr. Hamilton?"

"Huh?"

"Don't you have things to do?"

He fanned the stack of papers at me. "You'd be upset if I didn't mark these."

"No." I shook my head. "Not really." A braid had come loose. I braided it back.

I didn't feel like drawing today. I didn't feel like going home either. I felt more like talking. "Can I ask you something?"

He looked up. "You can hang up some prints I've been saving. Now that the bulletin board is empty, we can use it."

I frowned, but said I'd do it anyway. I covered the board with a bright yellow paper, then took a batch of pictures out of a brown folder.

Some of the pictures I really liked. In one, a lady was sitting on a couch next to two girls. They were dressed like twins in blue. A big Saint Bernard dog was lying down next to the couch. One girl was sitting on the dog!

"Who's this?" I asked. I put the picture on top of the papers he'd been marking.

"Uh . . . Madame Charpentier and her daughters. By Renoir. Now let me finish."

"Ren—— who?"

"Renior. He was an Impressionist."

"Why's it so fuzzy looking?" I asked.

"That's the technique the Impressionists used."

"Mm. I'm hanging this one up. Okay?"

49

He nodded, then went back to his work. I found another one in the folder. It was very different. You could see every line in the faces and the towel the lady dried the baby with.

"One last question," I said, showing him this picture. "This isn't by Renoir. I know."

"How do you know?" he asked, smiling. He knew I was trying to make him stop working, but I also wanted to know about these pictures. "Mary Cassatt did that one. The original is in The Art Institute of Chicago," he said.

"A lady artist in a museum?" I hardly knew there were any lady artists, period, let alone any in museums.

"Her work's in museums all over the world."

"Wow."

"She was born in the nineteenth century. She died in 1926."

"She was old."

"Uh-huh. She studied art in Philadelphia and ran away to Paris to paint."

"What about her mother and father, brothers and sisters?" I was wondering how she could love art more than her family. I tried to imagine loving something more than I loved Ma, Daddy, and Jason. I couldn't.

"She loved to paint. . . ."

"Like me."

"Like you. And in those days, it wasn't proper for a young lady to paint as a career. Her father was dead set against it."

"Boy, if my father told me not to draw, I might run away myself. How long does it take to get to Paris?"

He laughed. "I'm only halfway through these papers." Suddenly he got up and went to the folder. He took out a print of two ladies. One was sitting. The other was standing with an umbrella in her hand. "This is Mary Cassatt and her sister Lydia. It's by Degas."

"Daygah," I repeated. I liked the sound of the name. "A painter painting a painter." It was funny.

I could've stayed in the room for the rest of the afternoon putting up pictures and looking at them. Once in a while I imagined pictures of mine hanging somewhere. People came from all around to admire them. "That's an original Lorraine Maybe," they'd say.

"Won't your parents worry?" Wolfman asked. "It's almost four." He had his coat on and was carrying his black briefcase.

"My mother's busy. My father doesn't live with us."

"Oh," he said, as though he didn't know.

"He comes around from time to time."

"That's good. It's important to stay close."

"Only he doesn't come around that much."

"Talk to him if it bothers you," he said.

"You don't know him," I said. I got my books ready to take home.

"You ever tried?"

I shook my head. We left the empty school. We walked to his bus stop.

"Try it. You'd be surprised what talking things out can do."

Wolfman was right about a lot of things. He just might be right about this.

13

When I got home, Ma was there. I raced to the kitchen, throwing my knapsack and books down. "Guess what, Ma!"

Ma was bent over the table. She was pinning a pattern to some striped material. Pins, scissors, and all her stuff was spread all over the kitchen. She was so busy, she didn't answer me.

"Maaa!"

She looked up, surprised seeing me there. She kissed me.

"Guess what, Ma?"

Ma sighed. "Honey, I'm three weeks behind schedule. The spring fashion show is soon and . . ."

"But, Ma."

"Can't it wait?" Ma went back to pinning. The only choice I had was to wait.

"Nobody has any time," I said under my breath. I went looking for my knapsack. It had landed underneath the lamp table. I took out some Magic Markers and my drawing book. I made the drawing book during art the other day. The pages were still blank. I couldn't think of anything to put on them.

When I thought Ma must be finished, I went back into the kitchen. She still had five pieces to cut. One side of a suit was cut out. I held it up to me. "What do you think?" I twirled round and round like the models on TV.

"It's dragging on the floor," Ma said. "Put it down."

I dropped in the chair. "I'm hungry. Can I get pizza?"

Ma nodded, cutting slowly.

I stood on the stool to get the money can off the shelf in the cabinet. I was on my way out the door.

Ma called me. "Where do you think you're going, young lady?"

Ma must be going crazy. "To get pizza. You said . . ."

Ma shook her head. She gathered up scraps of material and put them in the garbage. "Not today. Not now. Your father's coming for you in a little while." She glanced at the clock on the wall.

"Why didn't you tell me sooner? When did he call?"

"This afternoon. Damn, he'll be here any minute."

Ma raced around. She threw open closets and drawers. She tossed Jason's and my clothes on the couch. She was like a speeded-up movie. It was crazy.

I called Jason from next door. "Go wash," Ma said.

"I already did once today. Is Daddy taking us for the whole entire weekend? And how come he can't call sooner?"

"He's busy. What can I tell you?"

"Why can't he call, though?"

Ma put her hand on her hip. "Do you want to go?"

I sighed, but said, "Yes."

"Act like it. Now, hurry up." She gave me a pat on the behind, sending me in the direction of the bathroom.

When I finished washing up, Jason dashed past me. "Daddy's coming," he said, all excited.

I ignored Jason and said to Ma, "I'll pack my own stuff." I kept my knapsack near the suitcase.

Ma gave me a curious look. "Something bothering you?" she finally asked.

"Not really." I laid a pair of blue jeans out flat. Then I put a shirt on top of them and rolled both of them together into one roll and put it in my suitcase. Each time I wanted to wear something, the whole outfit was in one place.

Ma kept watching me. She said, "Something is bugging you."

I didn't answer. But Ma could tell.

"Okay," I finally said. "How come Daddy didn't call yesterday?"

"For what?"

"To say he was coming. So we don't have to rush. So we know."

"Good question," Ma said. "You know how he is."

"Are we going with him every weekend, or what?"

Ma hunched her shoulders.

"See, we don't know nothing." I threw a roll in the suitcase.

"You want to go every weekend?" Ma asked. She sounded hurt.

"It's not that," I said in a hurry. But in a way, it was. I wanted to be with Daddy too. Two days a week wasn't a whole lot. And it just takes a minute to make a telephone call.

Ma sighed, relieved. "Then, don't complain so much and finish packing."

Complaining was dumb. At least I would have my own room.

"Underwear," Ma reminded me just as I was closing the suitcase.

"Dag!" I had to start all over again.

Ma gave me a whole stack of panties and undershirts. "All this for one weekend?" I asked, wishing I could leave those baby undershirts behind.

"Hurry up, please."

Jason threw his remote control racing car in his suitcase. Ma sat on Jason's to make it close.

A few minutes later, a car horn honked. "Daddy," Jason said, running to the window. He yelled, "Daddy's here."

Ma brushed lint off my coat, reminded Jason to zip up his pants and rebuttoned his coat. She kissed us and shoved us out the door. "Have a good time."

"You, too," I said, kissing her back. "I forgot to get something."

"Come back and get it."

"I can't remember." Even if I stood up there for a hundred years I wouldn't remember. "Ma?"

"Huh?"

"Send it to me if you find it." I was missing Ma already.

Ma smiled and said, "Sure."

"Last one downstairs is a rotten egg," Jason screamed. He looked ridiculous wobbling down the hall and dragging his suitcase on the floor.

"Dummy, you're going to *fall* downstairs and break your neck."

"Don't call your brother names. And Jason?"

"Huh?"

"Take your time. And behave yourself. I mean, both of you."

"Bye."

"Bye." She shut the door when she heard the outside door close.

Daddy bent down for me to kiss his cheek, then he picked up Jason, kissed and hugged him.

Jason hopped into the front seat next to Daddy. I slid in the back.

Ma waved at us from the window. A tape measure was hanging around her neck. Something about her standing there made me sure what I was leaving behind was very important.

Daddy drove away. "Who wants to pay the toll?" he asked when we got to the bridge.

"Me."

Over his shoulder he handed me seventy-five cents. What if one of the quarters bounced on the ground and Daddy busted through anyway? I wondered what would happen. All the quarters made the bucket.

"Oh, wow!" Jason's mouth hung open when the pole went up. "This is the Triboro Bridge, Lorraine," Jason said.

"I know that," I said. I'd read the name over the toll booths. Jason was smart about bridges and stuff. He didn't read books like normal people. He read maps. Train maps. Bus maps. Road maps. Any kind of map.

It took a long time to get to the restaurant. It was fun riding in the car and watching buildings flash by. But, then Daddy asked us about school. "Fine," I said. I looked out the window again.

Jason said, "Not so fine." I thumped him on his skull.

Daddy didn't know what to say. He asked us about school again.

"I got a hundred on spelling," Jason said.

"How about you, Lorraine?"

"Huh?" I had some questions to ask him.

"How are your grades?"

"Fine." How do you ask your father why he can't keep his promises?

I almost did. Then Daddy said, "This is it."

Daddy got off the highway. The restaurant looked like an old brown house sitting in the middle of nowhere.

We went inside. A lady took our coats. A little dish of quarters was on the counter.

"That must be for kids," Jason said, reaching.

"Dummy, those're her tips." I hit his hand. He hit me back.

"Kids! Be nice."

Inside the big room there were a lot of round tables and a lot of people, but it was so quiet it reminded me of a funeral parlor.

A short, round waiter took us to our table. I tiptoed all the way. The first thing I did when I sat down was put my hand over the candle. It was real warm.

The waiter handed us gold menus. They were taller than Jason.

"Get a load of those prices," I said. "What a gyp."

Daddy said, "Shhhh. You act like you've never been to a restaurant before."

"Not like this." I leaned over and whispered, "Remember that funeral parlor around our way? It had red lights too."

57

Daddy gave me that look. It was time to stop talking about funeral parlors.

The waiter asked, "Are you ready to order?"

"Kids?"

Jason said, "Lobster."

Daddy said, "You don't want lobster."

"I love lobster."

"Have you ever tasted it?"

"I still love it."

While Daddy and Jason fussed about the lobster, I tried the hand over the candle trick. There is a story in my reader about a man who eats fire, steps in it, and rubs his hands in it without ever burning himself.

"Stop that, Lorraine." Daddy knocked my hand away and frowned. He lit a cigarette. "Lobster's out."

"But I love it," Jason whined.

"Their beady eyes stare at you when you're eating them. Their claws'll grab your arm and yank it off," I said.

"Don't tell him those lies," Daddy said. "Only if they're alive can they hurt you."

"Then, I can have it?"

"No." Daddy shut his eyes, then opened them.

"Shall I come back when you're ready to order, sir?"

"Yes," I said.

"We're ready. Bring three chicken dinners."

"Do you have sardines?" I asked. I put the menu down.

The waiter sighed and said, "No. Now, we have roast chicken with stuffing, broiled chicken with mashed potatoes, or fried chicken in the basket, sir."

I noticed how he was talking to Daddy like Daddy was the only one at the table. "I'll take fried chicken with stuffing."

"Sir, she can only have it the way it's written on the menu. Fried chicken in the basket or . . ."

"Roast chicken is fine." Daddy handed the waiter all the menus. "Okay?"

"Yeah." Jason rubbed his hands together with a big grin. He'd eat even the beady eyes and claws of the lobster.

"Wait. What kind of stuffing comes with the chicken?" I was very polite and ladylike.

"Cornbread."

"Lorraine, if you don't like it when it comes, you don't have to eat it. Okay?"

"Well—as long as I still get dessert. Okay."

"Good." To the waiter Daddy said, "Bring me a double Scotch. Now."

Daddy gulped his whiskey down. He took out a pad and wrote a lot of numbers down. Jason was so busy leaning over his chair to see when the waiter was coming, he couldn't even play a game of Yours / Mine.

I placed my hand over the fire again just like the man in the book did. He can put his hand in fire for five whole seconds. I wasn't quite that brave. I just put mine an inch over it. Daddy was bored here with us. With me.

Daddy glanced up for a second, then wrote more numbers. He cursed under his breath.

One . . . two . . . three . . . "Awwww!" I screamed.

Daddy jumped up. "What's wrong?"

People at other tables were looking at us.

"The trick didn't work," I said, and I felt like crying.

"What trick?"

Jason laughed into his corner of the tablecloth.

"It's not funny, Jason." Daddy examined my hand.

59

The spot turned red and shiny. "What degree is it?" Jason asked.

"Waiter!" Daddy called.

I will not cry. I will not cry. It doesn't hurt that much.

I shook my hand until it almost dropped.

It's just a tiny burn. I will . . .

"Next time you'll leave fire alone," Daddy said.

The waiter brought me a bowl of cold water. I pushed my hand into it. I wanted to drown my hand. I licked the tears off my mouth and sniffed.

"Can we eat now?" Jason whined. "I'm dying of hungeravation."

People at the next table laughed into their bowls of spaghetti.

"That's starvation," Daddy said. "Starvation."

We finished eating, and the waiter brought the check on a silver plate.

"Was everything satisfactory?" the waiter asked, his hands behind his back.

"Uh . . ."

Daddy gave me a look and said, "Yes. It was very nice."

I had a whole list of things wrong, starting with that itty-bitty piece of chicken and ending with that hard-as-a-rock cake.

"I hope we don't eat out all the time," I said, and pushed the restaurant door wide open.

"Don't worry," Daddy said. This is the first and last time, he was probably thinking. Because of me.

Daddy stuffed his wallet into his pocket and pulled out the car keys. We walked to the parking lot.

"Next time," Jason said, "I'm going to get lobster."

"Lobster's too expensive," Daddy said.

Dag. Daddy thought about money all the time. Money. Money. Money. Money?!

I stopped in the middle of the lot. "My homework. I didn't bring it."

"Why not?" Daddy asked. "You should put important stuff in your knapsack where you won't lose it."

"That's just it. I put the important stuff in it. Homework won't fit."

Daddy sighed.

"We got to go back. I can't go on the trip if I don't turn the homework in." My stomach did a somersault. I was set to run all the way back to The Bronx. I hated to ask Daddy to drive back, but I did.

"By the time I drive you home and back, it'll be very late. And I'm tired. What I'll do is bring you back early Sunday."

"No," Jason said.

I didn't like that idea either. "Uh . . . no. I'll tell Mr. Hamilton what happened. He'll excuse me." He had to excuse me because we were going to the Metropolitan Museum of Art.

We got into the car.

"Now," Daddy said. "Are we ready to go?" He started the engine.

"Yes," I said. I stretched my legs across the back seat.

"I have to go to the bathroom," Jason said. "Real bad, too."

Daddy huffed. He banged on the steering wheel. He cursed to himself.

14

Wolfman called each person to his desk for the money to go to the museum. He called all the people at my table. He skipped right over me.

"Raise your hand. Quick," Nereida said.

"Wait. He's saving me for last."

"Why?" Rhonda asked.

"Just wait and see."

He called everyone in the room except Leroy and me. Leroy had no homework either. Wolfman took Leroy out the door.

"Here." Nereida gave me her homework to copy.

"Copy cat. Copy cat," Rhonda sang.

"Oh, shut up," I said. I copied so fast, my handwriting was like a chicken scratch.

"Copying is cheating. And . . ." Rhonda said.

"You got such a big mouth," Warren said. I was shocked he was sticking up for me. He didn't look so funny in those glasses just then.

"I'm the president. Remember?" Rhonda made the big announcement.

"Let's impeach her."

"Right."

"Raise your hands." All the hands shot up in the air. I was too busy copying to vote with the class. But enough kids voted to vote her out.

Instead of crying or being mad, Rhonda busted out laughing. "We change presidents tomorrow anyway."

Wolfman came back into the room. The class got quiet again. Under her breath, Rhonda said to me, "Cheating is against the law, for your information."

It didn't make any difference. I didn't have enough time to finish anyway.

"Please bring your things and come with me," he said.

"Who? Me?"

He nodded and took a deep breath.

Nereida moaned, "Oh, no. We can't be partners."

Ever since Nereida and me became friends again, we promised that we would always be partners, eat lunch together and walk home together. Now Wolfman was messing up the whole thing.

I got up feeling everyone watching, crossed the room, and followed him out the door. Wolfman closed the door. No one but us was in the hall.

"I was at my father's house. That's why I didn't do my homework." I crossed my fingers, hoping the truth was working.

He bit down on his lip and glanced down the long, empty hall. "I know you've been counting on seeing the Impressionists. But you didn't do your homework."

"I went to my father's in Queens."

"You could've taken your books with you."

"I forgot them at my mother's house."

He shook his head, scratching his beard at the same time.

"Please. See, I brought my lunch. My favorite lunch and money for souvenirs. See." I showed him my folded up dollar bill. "It's not like I see my father every day."

He scratched his beard. He must've been thinking.

Right away I said, "All the other kids live with their fathers."

He sighed. "Everybody had the same chance. And you're not so different from the other kids." He sighed again, looking down at me. "I'm sorry. There'll be other trips."

"You don't understand." My voice trembled. A lump got stuck in my throat. No more words came out.

"Mr. Hamilton?" Mrs. Dunbar called from her office. "Your bus is waiting. The driver is anxious to get on the way."

"Yes," he said. "We'll be down."

"I'll place Lorraine," she said. She went back in her office.

"Okay." Then to me, he said, "You go to the office. We'll talk when the class gets back."

"It'll be too late then. I want to go now."

He shook his head. "I couldn't explain it to the children who worked hard to get in all the back homework. I think you understand that."

I understood it all right, but I didn't like it. I went into Mrs. Dunbar's office and dropped down in one of the orange chairs parents usually sit in. She was on the telephone. She didn't say anything about me sitting there.

"I'm on my way down," she said, and hung up the phone. "Sorry, Lorraine. There's always an emergency."

Grown-ups always pretend to be sorry for something. "That's okay," I said. But it was lousy. Today was the last day for the special exhibit I was supposed to see.

"Let's see. Where are we going to place you," she sang as if she was moving a checker on the checkerboard. Grown-ups like to use kids like checkers, moving you any-which-a-way.

She read down the sheet that had *P.S. 129, School Organization* written across the top, and all the classes in the school written on the bottom. "You can go with Miss Crane."

"MISS CRANE!?" I backed away slowly.

"What on earth . . . ?" Mrs. Dunbar didn't understand. She wasn't the assistant principal when I was in fourth grade last year, but I thought everybody in the school knew how bad I'd done in Miss Crane's class. She'd put U's in everything on my record card.

"That's fourth grade," I finally said.

"Oh, don't worry about it. The younger children will like you. Let's go."

Ever since last year, I hadn't spoken to Miss Crane. If I passed her in the hall, I looked away. Now I had to spend the whole day in her room.

Mrs. Dunbar went in first. Miss Crane didn't walk over to us; she switched; keeping both hands in the pockets of her yellow smock. Her slick, black ponytail flung from side to side. I bet she'd have droopy skin if she took the rubber band off.

Even when Mrs. Dunbar and Miss Crane started talking, the class stayed quiet. All the kids sat in rows facing the green board. All the books were opened to the same page. There was a lot of writing on the board. Once in a while a kid looked up, but no one talked, and no one stopped doing the work. It was the same work I had last year. They must really be bored.

"She can't go on the trip," Mrs. Dunbar said.

Miss Crane lifted one razor-thin eyebrow and said, "Really?" She pretended to be surprised for Mrs. Dunbar.

"Have a good day, Lorraine," Mrs. Dunbar said before she left.

I didn't answer. I knew what kind of day it would be.

Miss Crane closed the door and shoved a worksheet at me. "Do you have a pencil?"

"No."

"Sit in the back," she said, and gave me a pencil.

It only took me ten minutes to finish the worksheet. I raised my hand to say I was finished.

She said, "Take a book and read."

The same books from last year were on the shelf. I found a skinny one I hadn't read.

The class was still writing when I finished the book.

"Take another one," she said. "Reading can't hurt you."

After the second book, I was sick of reading, especially since I was supposed to be on the trip. By now the class was probably in Manhattan.

"Sit still until the class is ready."

The chair was too hard to sit still in all morning. Wolfman lets us get up when we're working. He even lets us talk.

"Give me some paper," I said to the girl next to me.

Miss Crane said, "No talking."

I held up the paper to show her I wasn't really talking.

"No talking. Period. That's easy to remember."

I sucked my teeth.

A little while later, the girl next to me finished all her work. She asked me to show her what I was drawing.

"That's good. It looks just like Fred Flintstone. Can I have it?"

"Sure. But you better not talk." I kept an eye on Miss Crane. She didn't look up from what she was writing. I bet she never even heard of Impressionists.

"Thanks," the girl said. She turned to the girl in back of her. "Look, Rosa."

"Draw Snoopy for me," said Rosa.

I drew Snoopy, forgetting all about Crabby Crane. Then other kids asked me to draw something for them. I got excited. I was like a hero to them even though I was about their same height. There were two differences. I was older. I could draw anything they asked me to.

"Man, I don't know anybody who draws like you," Rosa said.

"Plenty of people draw better," I said. I was getting ready to tell her about the Impressionists when Miss Crane stood in front of the room and called on Felix to come to the board.

"Quick!" I motioned for them to put away their pictures.

Rosa dropped her paper. It landed on the floor two desks in front of hers. Miss Crane switched up the aisle. She called on me. I prayed not to get caught. I wondered if Degas or Renoir ever got caught drawing when they should have been doing syllabication.

"You're learning something this year," said Miss Crane after I divided *sensible* into three syllables.

67

When Miss Crane turned to the board again, Rosa got up to get the picture. But without turning around, Miss Crane said, "Bring the paper to me, Rosa."

Rosa stood there. "I won't ask you twice, Rosa." Rosa gave her the paper and sat back down.

I slid down in my seat, but there was nowhere for me to hide. My name was in the corner of the picture.

"Drawing? In my room? When you should be paying attention?"

"But—"

"There's no excuse."

It didn't matter to her that I drew real good or that I didn't have anything else to do. "But— Mr. Hamilton lets me draw when—"

"I'm not Mr. Hamilton."

I tried to explain.

"We have work to do." She ripped the paper into shreds.

"Please." I jumped up, but sat back down. It was too late. Miss Crane's blood red nails crushed the pieces of paper into a ball. She dropped the ball into the trash basket.

My stomach turned upside down. For the rest of the day it never went right side up again. It felt like Miss Crane had thrown me away. I wanted to yell at her, call her names, or run out of the room like I did last year when she made me mad. But I sat very still. So still my body quivered. After lunch, she gave the kids ten minutes of free time. I didn't budge or talk to anybody.

"We can do anything now," Rosa said to me.

"She's not going to get me in any more trouble."

When I felt like drawing, I traced pictures with my

finger. What she couldn't see, she couldn't throw away. Ha. Ha.

It was like two years in jail. The class finally came back at two-thirty. Wolfman came to get me.

When we were walking back to our room, he asked, "How did you make out."

"Terrible." I told him the whole story.

He said something under his breath. Then he said, "She's unreasonable."

"I agree. And you know what?"

"What?"

"I'm not going to miss any more trips. That's for sure."

We went inside. In every way my room was much better than Miss Crane's, with our plants, pictures, and activity centers. It even smelled sweeter with the coconut incense Wolfman burned sometimes.

Nereida was laughing and talking with Rhonda, Claribel, and Millie. They showed each other their postcards and souvenirs. Claribel was sitting at my desk. She moved over so I could get my books out.

"Sit with us," Nereida said. She made room for me in her chair.

"We want to tell you what happened in the Egyptian room," Millie said. The girls giggled.

"She didn't water the plants today," Rhonda said.

"So," Nereida said. "One day?"

I shrugged. "I didn't do it Friday either." My job was to take care of the plants. I had to do something right for a change.

When I finished watering the plants, I cleaned the board erasers, which was Leroy's job. But Leroy was in his seat playing drums on his desk. I should be like him

69

and not care about anything. I banged the erasers harder against the window gates.

"Lorraine," Wolfman called me to his desk.

I put the erasers back on the board and went over to him.

He smiled at me. "You've taken this in a mature way."

"Ha. I don't feel mature." I felt sick about being left out.

"I think you are very mature," he said. "So, I brought you this." He took a blue and white bag out of his desk. The bag had *The Metropolitan Museum of Art* written on it. "Open it."

I opened it. Inside was a magazine about the special exhibit the class had seen. All the pictures were done by Degas. It cost $2.95. Even though I was glad to get the magazine, it made me sadder. I could've seen all these pictures live. "Thanks a lot," I said.

I showed the magazine to the girls. Rhonda snickered and said, "Heh. Heh. The teacher's pet."

I looked at Wolfman, waiting for him to say I wasn't the teacher's pet. He didn't. He smiled and said, "Time to go home."

To think that of all the kids in the class, I was the teacher's pet. I was so happy about the book, I showed Ma when she got home.

"I'm going to copy all the pictures in it, too," I said.

"That's a good idea," Ma said. She opened up her textbooks to study. "By the way," she said, looking up from the book, "I had a talk with your father. He's coming Saturday at twelve o'clock sharp."

15

Jason twisted and turned. He rolled right off the bed with a thump. He didn't wake up. I climbed on top of the bed and jumped. The bedsprings creaked, cranked, and creaked. I threw the pillow at his head. He knocked the pillow off him and started flinging his arms to get untangled from the covers.

"Get up! Don't you know what day it is, chicken butt?"

"Huh? What?" He stood up, looking around as though he'd traveled to another planet during the night.

I went back into the kitchen where Ma was frying the sausage for breakfast. She was humming. The sun blasted through the window. Even inside the house, it was easy to tell it was the beginning of spring. Less heat came up on the radiator. No one banged for more.

"Is Jason woke?" Ma asked. She cracked the eggs on the side of the bowl.

"It's time to take the biscuits out," I said. I opened the oven door. "Yep. They're done."

"Did you throw the pillow at him again?" Ma asked.

"The pot holder. Where is it?" The pot holder was hanging on its nail over the sugar and flour cans. I looked around for it anyway.

"The same place it always is. And I told you a thousand times not to do that to him."

"He won't wake up when I just call him."

"Honestly." Ma sighed. "How would you like someone to jump on the bed, yell, scream, and throw pillows at you when you're dead asleep?"

If I kept up the argument, Ma would give me a lecture. Who needed lectures on Saturday morning! So I finally said, "I wouldn't like it." I took the biscuits out.

"I didn't think so." Ma put the carton of eggs back into the refrigerator.

Jason finally came in. He was washed and dressed. He rubbed the sleep out of his eyes. Ma beat all the eggs together. All of us ate our eggs scrambled. Everybody except Daddy. "What time is Daddy coming?" I asked.

Jason yawned.

"Twelve. I told you," Ma said.

"Can I call to make sure?" I asked.

"Eat first."

I rushed through my favorite breakfast to beat Jason to the phone. He loved to dial. He also loved to run his mouth. If I didn't get there first, I wouldn't get a chance to ask Daddy about us playing in the backyard of his building. He promised that on the first warm Saturday, we could spend the whole day out there. It wasn't anything like the ones around here. There were swings, slides, a hopscotch court painted on the ground, places to jump rope and play ball. Not a piece of garbage, not even a candy wrapper was anywhere.

"I'm finished," I said, getting up.

Jason said, "Me, too."

I pushed him aside and grabbed the phone. He punched me. "Ha, ha. It didn't hurt." I dialed the number at the garage. The phone rang seven times before anyone picked it up.

A man with a deep voice answered.

"Can I speak to my father. He's James Maybe."

The man yelled, "Yo! Jake. It's your kid." Then he said in a quieter voice, "He'll be here." He laid the receiver down.

I waited a long time.

Jason pulled on my new sweater. He asked, "What's taking so long?"

"Maybe he forgot," I said. I called Daddy's name into the phone. Maybe someone would hear me. But no one came. A lot of talking was going on in the background. Car horns honked. Dogs were barking. It was a busy Saturday. Daddy had promised to take part of the day off. I wondered if he still intended to.

"What are you yelling about?" Daddy asked finally.

"Hi, Daddy," I said, glad he had come at last.

Jason reached for the phone. "Give me. I want to say hello too."

I put my hand over the phone and said, "Wait." I turned my back to Jason. "Daddy, Ma wants to know if you're still coming at twelve o'clock because we're ready now."

"Leave it!" Daddy yelled.

"What?"

"Not you." He was talking to one of his workers. "I was going to call you. It's a madhouse today. Seems like

73

everybody in Queens has a broken-down car. I'll be working all night."

I swallowed. I knew what that meant.

"Is he coming at twelve?" Jason asked.

I ignored him. Daddy was still telling me the reasons why he couldn't come today. "When I *get* the time to drive all the way up to The Bronx, it'll be very late."

I bit my lip. "I know the way. Ma can put me and Jason on the right subway. I promise we won't get lost. And I'll watch Jason real good."

At first, Daddy didn't say anything. Then he said, "It'll mean you all sitting in my office all day." We were used to doing that anyway. Daddy would give us a handful of quarters to buy hot chocolate and candy out of the machines. Two cups of chocolate and I was ready to throw up. I ended up saving the quarters.

"That's okay," I said.

Daddy yelled out again. I don't even think he was listening. "Coming, man. Hold on." He breathed out. "Look, Lorraine. I got to go now. See you next week. It's a promise."

"But what about today?" I asked.

Jason grabbed the phone before I heard Daddy's answer. "Hi, Daddy," Jason said. He blinked. He hung up the phone. "Daddy already hung up."

"That figures," I said. I went back into the kitchen where Ma was. Her material was laid out on the table. I said, "Daddy's not coming."

She folded the material back up. "Then, let's go shopping."

"How come Daddy's busy *all* the time?" Jason asked.

We both looked at Ma for the answer. She didn't have an answer. If she did, she wasn't telling us.

She finally said, "He's always been that way. Work. Work. Work."

"Maybe we're just pains in the necks," I said.

Jason said, "I'm not."

Ma hugged him. "Of course you're not. Lorraine isn't either." She added my name because I was standing there. "How about shopping?" she asked again. "You've wanted those shoes for a long time."

"I don't feel like it," I said.

"I may not have extra money next week."

"I don't want any dumb old shoes. Can I go play?"

Ma sighed. "First you want them, and then you don't. . . ."

How can new shoes make up for now? Ma should understand. "Can I go play?" I asked again.

Ma threw up her arms and said, "All right. Just don't go far."

I put on my jacket. Jason put on his too and tagged behind me. On the way downstairs, he asked, "We going to play in the lot?"

"No. Who wants to play in garbage?" Ever since I saw what a really nice place to play looked like, I hated the vacant lots around here. There weren't any treasures buried anywhere. It was all trash. When it rained, the trash smelled like rotten fish.

I sank down on the stoop. My behind froze on the cold step. But, so what. I stayed right where I was.

"That's mine," Jason hollered when a green car came up the street. A red one came up. He hollered, "That's mine," again. He pulled my arm. "You're not playing."

I knocked his hand away. "Leave me alone."

"But I want to play." He was whining like a big, snotty-nosed baby.

75

"So. Nobody stopping you. Just leave me alone. Go play with somebody your own age."

Nobody we knew was outside playing. Some boys were playing stickball in the middle of the street. We weren't allowed in the middle of the street. A lot of kids were probably over in Crotona Park. We weren't allowed there either. And Jason couldn't go anywhere alone. Not even to the store. So I guess I was being a little unfair to him. So I played a game of Yours / Mine until Jason had won eight shiny new cars and I had won three beat-up jalopies.

Even while I was playing the game, I kept thinking about Daddy. In one way, I absolutely believed what I was thinking. In another way, it didn't make sense. I asked Jason.

"That's the dumbest thing I ever heard. Daddy do so love us."

"How do you know?" He was so sure. Maybe I was only imagining things.

"Easy," Jason said. "He's our father. Fathers have to love their kids."

"Why?"

"That's the rule. Isn't it?"

I sucked my teeth and rested my head in my hands. That was the big problem. Jason's answer was the same as mine. All fathers loved their kids. But it seemed that our father didn't. Maybe nobody told him the rules. Maybe he knew the rules and didn't care about them.

"Isn't it?" he asked again. This time he wasn't so sure.

"It's the rule. But maybe we're not following the rules either."

"Huh?"

"You know, like being good all the time and showing

76

Daddy we really love him. If we did that, he'd love us back."

"And . . ." Jason's eyes lit up as though a thousand thoughts were coming to him. "And, and, he'll come back to live with us."

I shook my head. "Nah. Ma don't want him to live with us, I don't think."

He punched me. "Don't say that."

I had to say it because that was true. "Remember before they broke up, Jason? They were always fighting. Daddy would go out and slam the door?"

"So what."

"So what? Ma'd end up crying. She don't cry now, Jason. She's smiling and singing."

Jason wagged his head from side to side. It didn't matter if he believed me or not. Getting Daddy to come back home wasn't our problem.

We went back upstairs for a few minutes. To go to the bathroom for one thing. And to get paper and a pencil.

Ma took a bunch of pins out of her mouth. "Going to play ball?"

"Ball?" I asked. "Yes, we're going to play ball. Get the ball, Jason."

Jason got the ball without a word.

Ma said, "Lunch will be ready in half an hour."

"Okay," I said.

"See you later, Ma," Jason said.

Ma came to the door to watch us out. She always did.

"Ma, I'm too big for you to watch out," I said.

"You didn't complain a little while ago."

"I know. But twice in a day is too much," I said.

Ma didn't watch us out. It was kind of scary in the hall.

77

If a mugger was on the steps, Ma wouldn't be at the door ready to save us.

But what was more scary than going two flights down to the street, was going four flights up to the roof. And that's where we were going.

16

I tried the elevator on the third floor. It was still out of order. We had to walk all the way up. It was the only place we could go that was private. Until summer no one went up there. Then, people came up to mess with their pigeons.

"Suppose a mugger hits us over the head," Jason said.

"Wouldn't be any muggers up there this time of the year. A mugger would starve to death waiting on somebody to come up there."

"We going."

"But he don't know that. Now be quiet."

When we got to the sixth floor, Jason threatened to turn around and go back. The hall lights were blown out. We couldn't see anything.

After we'd come this far, I wasn't going all the way back down. Besides, this was important. "Hold on to me. Okay? And walk up against the wall. Nothing will happen. I promise."

"It's too dark. I can't even see myself."

"You can't see yourself if it's light. So what's the difference? Don't be a scaredy-cat. Come on." I grabbed his hand and held it tight. My hand was sweating too. But I didn't let on that I was a little scared. Then Jason would be more scared.

I felt my way along the cold, bumpy wall until I came to an apartment door. The door was smooth, and I felt the place where the bell was. A dog barked. Jason's hand stiffened.

"It must be Mrs. Brown's dog." I gulped. "She's in 6E. Right?"

"I think so."

"The steps are right over there. Let's get away from this door." I pulled Jason along. The dog kept on barking.

I was at the steps to the roof. I took hold of the bannister. But my sox had crawled down into my sneakers. I let go of Jason's hand for one second.

"Don't let go," he screamed.

"Mrs. Brown's going to hear you."

"But don't let go." His voice went back to a whisper.

"I'm sorry." I took his hand. "It's fifteen steps, I think. Count with me."

A crack of light escaped through the door. There was no lock on it. "It's just a piece of wire," I told Jason. "I'm going to let your hand go for a minute just so I can undo the wire."

I only stuck myself three times untwisting the wire. Finally I pulled it through the hole where the lock should have been. I pushed the door open and we stepped out.

"Man, this's like heaven," Jason said.

I'd never seen so much sky either. It was all stretched

out. For as far as I could see, there was blue sky and white fluffy clouds here and there. Looking downtown, I could even see the top of the Empire State Building.

The floor of the roof was mushy soft and black. I kicked a rusty beer can out of my way. "It's filthy even up here," I said.

"You said it."

The pigeon coop stood on the far side of the roof. It was put together with wood and wire. No birds flapped around. The door swung with the wind.

Jason leaned over the edge of the roof. "Oh, boy, I can see Mr. Santiago's window. His cat's eating the plants."

I grabbed Jason and pulled him away. "We're going to sit over here by the chimney." We sat down and I took out the pencil and paper.

"We going to write?" He asked as though he'd just swallowed a tablespoon of milk of magnesia. "I want to go play with Julio."

"Sit still." I pushed him back down. "What's more important—this or Julio's trains?"

Jason put his finger to his head, thinking it over.

I knocked his finger down. "This is." I gave him a sheet of paper. "Now, write down all the things we have to do."

"For what?"

"So Daddy can love us." I swallowed.

"I don't want to, because he does."

"Then why doesn't he keep his promises and visit us and stuff?"

Jason hunched his shoulders. He played in a little pile of dirt next to him.

"No," he said, and threw the paper away. The wind

81

carried it off the side of the building. "This is dumb. I want to go home."

"It's not dumb," I said.

Jason folded his arms across his chest.

"Dag. I'll do the writing."

He looked over.

"Your writing's not too good anyway."

"It is so." He unfolded his arms and sat up straight.

"No, it's not. Besides, you threw away your paper. We'll just use one sheet."

On the top of the page, I wrote *Ways To Make Daddy Love Us.* "I'll start."

"Why you?"

"Because I'm older than you are."

A lot of things came to my mind. So many, it was easy to see what the problems were. "First thing is we have to stop acting up around the garage."

"I don't act up."

"You do so."

"Who tried to set the dogs loose?"

"All right. *I* promise not to act up." I wrote it down. Only I kept in the *we.* "And we won't complain about the hot chocolate being too sweet."

"I never did." Jason bit a fingernail and spat it out.

"This'll take all day if you pick on every single word I say."

"Tell the truth, then."

"I'm trying to. But if I said, 'I, I, I,' Daddy would end up loving me more than you. Do you want that to happen?"

"Uh . . . uh," said Jason, shaking his head.

After we finished the list, I wrote it into a letter.

Dear Daddy,

We are sorry for being bad. We don't mean to be. We promise not to do any of the things that get on your nerves.

1. We promise not to ask for a puppy anymore.
2. We won't miss the toll bucket on purpose just to see if the cops will chase us.
3. We won't mess in your desk anymore. We didn't know the top on that bottle of ink was loose.
4. We won't ask for lobster anymore. We'll eat what's on our plates.
5. Even if you don't call first, we'll be ready when you come for us. We won't remind you about the movies or the pizzeria.
6. We'll try not to throw up out the car window.
7. It's okay if you don't come at 12:00 sharp.
8. It's a good idea not to drive a car until we are 18 years old. We won't try out the old cars you're fixing.

> Signed,
> Your children, Jason and Lorraine

P.S.
If all these things come true, you will love us. Right?

After I read the letter to Jason, he said, "You should make number 9, 'We'll be good boys and girls.'"

"*Brother.* You come up with one idea, and it's dumb."

"It's not dumb." Jason argued with me while I put it in the envelope I'd brought, all stamped, and all the way down to the sixth floor.

"Shhh . . ."

Mrs. Brown's dog was barking like crazy. Just as we walked past the door, it opened. The dog shot into the hall. He ran up to us, then back to his door. We stood frozen.

"Rusty, what you bawlin' about?"

"Mrs. Brown," I whispered to Jason.

Mrs. Brown locked her door. "Somebody's out here." She switched on her flashlight. The light blinded me.

"We live downstairs. Take that light away," I said.

"What you doin' up here if you live downstairs?"

"Make your dog stop barking," I begged.

"Can't," she said.

So Rusty kept on barking and sniffing at us. Mrs. Brown stood there with the flashlight shining on us. "What I'm goin' to do with you all," she said as though she was thinking of something mean and awful.

Just then the roof door swung open. Rusty dashed up the stairs.

"Rusty! Rusty!" she called. Rusty finally trotted over to her. "You all been up on that roof. Playin'."

"No, ma'am. We weren't playing," I said, shaking.

"Don't you know what happens up there?" She shook the flashlight in my face.

Jason nudged me. "Show her the letter."

No way was I going to show it to crazy Mrs. Brown. "It's private. And we have to go now. Come on, Jason," I said slowly. We walked down the first flight of stairs. Mrs. Brown's eyes were on us.

But as soon as we were down to our floor, we ran the rest of the way. We didn't stop running until we got to the mailbox at the corner.

I turned the envelope over to double-check Daddy's

address. All of a sudden, Jason snatched the envelope from me and dropped it through the slot.

"Satisfied?" I asked, angry at him.

But by the wide grin on his face, I could tell he was. He put his arm around me. I put mine around him.

When we saw Mrs. Brown walking Rusty, she asked Jason, "Like ginger snaps?" She held out one to Jason like he was an old friend.

I knocked Jason's hand away as he was about to take it. I pushed him up the block.

"How come I couldn't take it?" Jason asked, poking his fat lip out.

"We have enough problems without getting mixed up with her."

But at least one of our problems was just solved.

17

Every day I raced home to check the mail. While I waited for Daddy to call, I did my homework and drew pictures from the magazine Wolfman had given me. The time went by faster. Before I knew it, Ma'd be home. It was time for dinner. And Daddy still hadn't called.

Jason leaned over me, watching me draw. "How long does a letter take?"

"A day. Sometimes two or three." I didn't look up from the picture I was doing. It was the picture Degas had painted of Mary Cassatt and her sister, Lydia. In the magazine, the picture was in black and white. I put in my own colors.

"It's been a week." He counted the days on his fingers.

"Not a week," I said. "It's been five days."

"So then, five is long enough time."

I put the green Magic Marker in the box and took out a purple one. "Maybe Daddy's out of town. He goes to lots of meetings and stuff."

"Let's call and see."

"Not now. I need to finish this first." Besides, I was scared Daddy was right in his shop and had gotten our letter days ago. Suppose he read it, laughed, threw it away, then forgot all about us?

"No, you don't need to finish it now. Let's call."

"No."

"I'll do it myself." Jason dialed the phone. "Hi, Daddy. How come you didn't answer our letter?"

"Stupid," I said under my breath. "Starting off like that." I took the phone from him. The letter could've gotten lost in the mail. I could've written the wrong address on the envelope. Jason had snatched it from me before I checked. My heart thumped real loud. I swallowed. "Hello," I said.

"Hi." Daddy sounded happy.

"How was your trip?"

"Trip! You kidding! I've been living and sleeping in this place. I'm going to need a trip before this week is out."

Boy, that was a relief. We sent the letter to his house. No wonder he didn't get it.

Jason yelled into the phone, "Did you get our letter?"

I pushed him away.

Daddy said, "Tell Jason it came in the mail the other day. I was going to give you a call later."

I put my hand over the phone. "He said he was going to call later," I said to Jason.

Jason said, "Now he don't have to."

"What's up?" Daddy asked.

"Nothing. You said . . . about the letter?"

"It was a funny thing to write." Daddy laughed. "I'm your old man. Remember? You don't have to ask me if I love you. Right?"

Jason reached for the phone again. I was about to give

87

it to him. Daddy said, "Lorraine? Lorraine? I thought you hung up."

"No, I'm here. Jason wants to talk."

Jason took the phone. I took my painting things into the kitchen. I closed the door. It was quiet except for the ice defrosting in the refrigerator. I finished painting the skirts on Lydia. It was an old-timey skirt. But I made it look nice with yellow and brown diamonds going down the side. Before I hang it on the wall in the living room, I'll show Wolfman.

"I've been calling you," Jason said, coming into the kitchen.

"What?"

"Daddy said to come and say good-bye."

"No." I decided to put black diamonds in the skirt too.

"Guess what. Our plan worked." I looked up. "Daddy promised to be on time next week."

"That'll be the day." I went back to drawing. A lot of pictures I wanted to draw were in my head. The more I thought about them, the less I thought about Daddy's promises.

18

I was voted the class treasurer in May. Warren nominated me. I couldn't believe it. Claribel, Michael, and I were sent out of the room. I was sure either Claribel or Michael would win. But they didn't. I got the most votes. Then I nominated Nereida to be president, and she won. Rhonda got mad. She didn't win anything. Nobody nominated her for anything, either.

"You think you're so special," she said to me on the way down to lunch. "Being treasurer is a dumb job."

"So," I said. "It's better than being nothing."

Nereida laughed. Rhonda made a face.

In the lunchroom, Nereida and I made sure we sat as far from Rhonda as we could.

I split my sardine sandwich with Nereida; she split her salami with me. She looked down to where Rhonda was eating all alone. "I feel sorry for her," Nereida said.

"How come?" I stuffed my mouth with the salami, then washed it down with strawberry milk.

"She don't know how to be friends," Nereida said. "She don't have any sisters or brothers either."

"It's her own fault. Nobody asks her to start trouble."

"Well, hurry up. Lunch'll be over soon." Nereida took her tray and dumped it.

I dumped my tray, picked up the jump rope and followed her out to the yard. We were having a double Dutch contest. We picked a spot in the yard that was away from all the noise and kids.

We shot odds / evens.

"We're first," I said.

I counted as Nereida jumped. "One. One-ten. One-twenty. One-thirty. One-forty."

The rope tangled up in her foot. She was out.

Claribel jumped the best. She turned around, stooped to the ground and jumped on one foot even. On her first try she went all the way up to four-fifty. Millie was her partner. She only got the score to five. She didn't jump so good. I had a chance to pull our score up to about three-thirty. We just might win. It was my turn to jump in when Rhonda walked over. She wanted to play.

"We're playing sides," I said.

"It's not your rope," she said.

"This one is mine," I said, showing her how the ends were worn out.

Nereida got in between us. "Wait till we switch the game." She was almost begging Rhonda to be fair.

"How long?" Rhonda asked, like she had a right to play with us.

Claribel said, "Three rounds. Lorraine, you're going to lose your turn. Hurry up."

"Okay." But Rhonda was standing right where I wanted to jump in from. I asked her to move.

"I'm not in your way," she said.

"You are too. Move. I got to jump in from *here*." She didn't budge. "I'm going to lose my turn."

"So."

"Please, move," Nereida said.

"Don't beg," I said.

Rhonda rolled her big eyes and tapped her foot. I pushed her out of the way.

She pushed me back. When I pushed her a second time, she stumbled backwards. When she got her balance back, she came at me swinging her arms.

"You're going to get it now," she said.

I swung my arms at her, grabbed her hair.

"Fight. Fight." Kids were shouting and running toward us.

Somehow we ended up on the ground, punching, scratching each other.

"Stop it. Stop it," Nereida screamed. Some kids tried to pull us apart. But I was really holding on to Rhonda.

"Let them fight."

"Wow—wee."

"She is getting jacked up."

Someone pushed through the crowd of kids. Light broke into the dark circle. "Break it up," a man said. He pulled me off Rhonda. Her nose was bleeding.

"Go play," another man said to the kids. But they didn't leave. He took Rhonda inside; the other one took me.

A bunch of kids followed us to the door, but left when we went inside. Nereida stayed with me.

"Where do you think you're going?" one man asked Nereida. I looked at him for the first time. It was the same aide who broke up the fight between me and Nereida.

91

"This is her sweater. And I know what happened," Nereida said.

"You go outside." He took the sweater, and Nereida left.

I took my sweater from him.

"You never know when to stop, do you?" he asked.

"Just don't touch me," I said. He didn't.

I walked into the office behind Rhonda and the other man.

Mrs. Barretto was sitting at her typewriter. When she saw Rhonda's bloody nose, she jumped up and got some ice and paper towels.

"What happened to you?" she asked. She wrapped the ice in the paper towel and put it to Rhonda's nose. The aide who brought her in left.

"She started it," Rhonda said.

"Liar!" I said.

The aide who brought me in said to Mrs. Barretto, "This one is always fighting." Mrs. Barretto looked at me and shook her head.

"I am not 'this one.' I have a name."

"Sit there," the aide said.

"No. I don't have to. It wasn't my fault."

He pushed me down on the bench. "Sit there."

I jumped up again. "Make me."

He pointed his finger at me. His eyes were two narrow slits. "You're going to get suspended."

I sat down. The door to the principal's office opened. If the principal came out, I probably would be suspended.

But the principal did not come out. I relaxed a little. It was Mrs. Dunbar. The man rushed to her and told her the whole story. Naturally, his side wasn't the whole truth. Mrs. Dunbar nodded, looking from Rhonda to me.

"We'll inform their teacher. He'll take care of it." When the man left, Mrs. Dunbar came over to me. "I'm surprised at you. Such a nice girl." Someone in the office grunted. I didn't know who. Mrs. Dunbar wrote something down on a piece of paper. She said, "Fighting can't be allowed."

I stared down at my untied shoelaces. A drop of blood from Rhonda's nose had soaked into my sneaker. I twisted that foot in back of the other, wishing I could forget.

"And, you," she said to Rhonda.

Rhonda took the ice pack off her nose and said, "She started it."

"Regardless of who started it," Mrs. Dunbar said, "it's a serious matter. I'll talk to Mr. Hamilton. Now go to your room. And absolutely no fighting on the way up. Understood?"

I said, "Yes." Rhonda nodded.

We went up separate staircases. It was Rhonda's idea. To stay far from me and stay out of trouble. But I wasn't thinking about her now.

Soon after we got upstairs, Mrs. Dunbar sent for Wolfman. He came back and hardly said a word to us all afternoon. He did something he had never done before. He gave the entire class a written punishment because when he told everyone to stop talking, nobody did. They were all mumbling about what was going to happen to Rhonda and me. This was the first time we had shared anything, even anything awful.

When it was time to go home, he called me to his desk. "T—Take this home," he said. He held out a long white envelope. It looked serious because *To The Parents of Lorraine Maybe* was typed across the front.

"What's this for?" I asked, putting my hands behind my back.

"Just take it home."

I grabbed the letter. Boy, he was a liar. He said he didn't like punishments, but the one he gave the class lasted all afternoon. And he told me once that he'd never suspended anybody.

"What if I tear it up?" I said.

"Lorraine—" He started to say something, but I walked back to my seat.

I said to Nereida, "I hate that teacher. And you want to know something?"

"What?"

"I don't care if he suspends me forever," I said loud enough for him to hear.

"Oooo," some of the kids said.

Nereida hit my foot. "Hey, look, Rhonda's going up, too."

"But I didn't do anything," Rhonda was saying. She sounded like she wanted to cry. The big crybaby.

But after I thought about it for a minute, I felt like crying myself. Being put out of school at ten years old was something to cry about.

"Make sure you girls copy your homework," he had the nerve to say. "And I prepared this packet of work."

I left the thick package of worksheets and books right where he laid it. If I wasn't coming to school, what was the sense in doing the homework?

At three, when the bell rang, I told everybody, "No, I am not suspended. I'll be here Monday morning. Wait and see."

19

All the way home I racked my brain. I couldn't figure out what to do with the letter so Ma wouldn't find out. I wasn't as good as I used to be about these things. Besides, sooner or later Ma would find out, especially when I told her I couldn't go to school Monday.

"Is that you Lorraine?" Ma called from the kitchen.

"Uh-huh." I didn't want to go in, but she called me.

She stopped pressing a dress to kiss me. "Want a snack?"

I shook my head.

"You know where I went today?" Ma asked. She was carefully pressing the dress, so she couldn't look at me. I was glad she didn't see my face.

"Uh-uh."

"Well"—she took a breath—"I saw the costume exhibit at the Met. And I just happened to pass the information desk. To make a long story short, read those papers on the chair."

"Ma."

"Read them, honey."

I shrugged. The first paper I picked up had a bunch of words on it. I put it down. The second one didn't have too many. I read it. "What does it have to do with me?" I asked.

"Wouldn't you like to take art workshops this summer?"

I must've looked pretty miserable. Ma said, "You can't go now. You spend the weekend with your father. Besides, July's not so far away." Ma smiled. "Excited, huh?"

I forced a smile.

I wanted to get excited about the art workshops and maybe forget about the letter. Maybe it would disappear if I stopped thinking about it. Why couldn't Mr. Hamilton use the mailbox? Why did he have to trust me to give it to Ma? Didn't he know I never gave Ma letters that were sent home? Even about little stuff. Like the time I took all the thingumajigs out of the basketballs, or when the class went to the Coney Island Aquarium and I left them and took the subway home by myself? Ma never got those letters. She found out everything at Parents' Night. I was stuck in the house for a month. Plus I got a beating.

How come he trusted me? To be mean enough to suspend me, he should've been mean enough to send the letter. That way I wouldn't be reaching into my bag fidgeting among my drawing books, Magic Markers. The letter.

"What's this?" Ma asked, slitting the envelope open with her finger.

"A letter. From Mr. Hamilton."

Ma looked at me, confused. As she read, her eyebrows

went up, then down. "Damn, Lorraine. Your explanation better be good."

It was a dumb fight. And a dumb reason.

"Well?" Ma said, her hand on her hip.

I explained about the jumping. A couple of times, and it sounded stupid. I stopped because of the lumps that kept sticking in my throat. "But, Ma, did he say I was bright and talented too?" I asked quickly. "He tells me that all the time."

Ma huffed. "This takes the cake."

"This means I can't have the art classes?"

"Suspended! Over a silly fight." Ma glared. "What do *you* think?"

"Rhonda keeps bugging me." I sucked my teeth.

"Bugging you! Bugging you!"

"She does."

Ma mumbled something, then raised her hand to hit me. I covered my head and screamed. But for some reason, she didn't hit me. After about a second or two, I uncovered my head. Ma was pinching her eyebrows together.

"I'm sorry, Ma."

Ma waved me off. "Go away, now. Do your homework till dinner."

"But, Ma."

Ma shut her eyes real tight.

"Never mind." On second thought, it was better not to tell her I left the homework in school.

Dinner went bad too. Ma put on some leftovers.

"Beef stew. Yuk," Jason said.

"Stop complaining and eat," Ma said.

97

"But I don't like this stuff even when it's just cooked," he said. He shoved his green peas to one side of his plate and mashed them up.

I moaned after each bite. But I was in too much trouble to complain about dinner. I might not get off easy this time. But even Ma frowned at the mush in front of her. She pushed her plate away and hid her face in her hands.

"It's not that bad," I said, forcing the stew down my throat without a sound. I ate every bit.

But not Jason. He asked, "Why can't we ever have lobster? Daddy . . ."

"Ha. Don't let on that Daddy feeds us better. He feeds us just as bad. I mean . . ."

Ma started to clear the table, nervously. "Finish up. And get your things ready."

"What time's he coming?" Jason asked. He raked his food in the garbage.

"About seven."

But seven o'clock came without a sign of Daddy. Then about seven-thirty, the phone rang. I answered it. It was him.

"H—Hi."

"Let me speak to your mother," he said in a hurry.

"Maaa."

Ma came to the phone. First Daddy did a lot of talking. Ma finally said, "Of all the times." She told him about me. "Honestly, I expect you to talk to her. No, I'm not beating her. . . . Talk. . . . Show concern. . . . For one thing, she brought it home herself. . . . That's right. . . ." Ma sighed. "Hold on."

Ma gave me the phone. "Hello," I said.

Daddy forgot to say hello again. "Why didn't you tell me about this letter?"

"You asked to speak to Ma. Are you going with her to the meeting?"

"Impossible."

"But . . . the meeting's for both of you. You got to come."

"It's too late to cancel my plans. Everything's paid for."

"Where're you going?"

"The Bahamas, for a long-needed rest."

"But, Daddy, this is serious."

He grunted. "The suspension's for how long? A week? Two?"

"Three days."

"And three days is not serious. You just better be glad it's not longer. Nobody has time to run to that school all the time."

What's he talking about? He never went. Ma went by herself. He never seemed interested in what teachers said. He was always too busy, too tired, or didn't feel like being bothered. He didn't even go to hear the good stuff.

"Look, I can't. That's it. You hear me?"

"Yes. I hear you." I gave the phone back to Ma. Daddy was still talking to me. But it didn't matter.

"Honey," Ma said. I stomped out and slammed the door.

Ma started fussing with Daddy. So I took out a drawing book and shut out the whole thing.

"Daddy on his way?" Jason asked. He was packing.

I felt terrible watching him pack to go nowhere. But I couldn't tell him. I might end up telling him the real reason why Daddy wasn't coming. I just grumbled, "I don't know."

I flipped through my Metropolitan Museum of Art

magazine, thinking how it's weird. Wolfman's not even related to me, and he got me one of the best presents I ever had. These three days, I was going to miss him. I found a picture I hadn't done yet, of ballet dancers in a rehearsal room. In June, we would be going to a ballet. Wolfman promised. We probably would.

"Jason," Ma said cheerfully when she came out of the bedroom. "How about Monopoly? I feel ready for you tonight."

Jason looked up from his packing. His eyes were big with worry. "We not going with Daddy?"

"Not this week. Daddy's going away." Ma got out the Monopoly. After Jason landed on the B. & O. Railroad, he played like he usually did—like his life depended on him buying up every other railroad and utility company. After that, he figured he'd won the game.

Ma unpacked for Jason once he was in bed and asleep. "You unpacked?"

"I never packed in the first place." I kept on drawing.

She took the drawing book from me. "My artist." She shook her head. She smiled as she flipped through the book. She put it down and said, "Time for bed."

When I got in bed, she tucked the covers under me. It's been a long time since I let her tuck me in. But it was okay for tonight. She sat down next to me. "I know what you're thinking about your father. He's not a bad guy, you know."

"Then how come he can't come to the meeting? All for a lousy trip?"

"The trip has nothing to do with it. That's his way. Just like his father. He thinks his duty stops with providing food and clothing. And it's *my* job to take care of the rest. Not that I mind."

"But, Ma." My voice was high and trembling. "What if I can't go back to school? Ever?"

"You will." Ma hummed and braided one of my braids. "As terrible as it is, it's not the very worst that can happen." She sighed. "You have work?"

"I left it on the teacher's desk." I thought maybe she'd hit me.

"I'll get it when I go to see him," said Ma.

I raised up on one elbow. "Tell me something, Ma."

"Hmmm?"

"Be honest?"

She nodded.

"Okay. If, say, I lived with Daddy, and say, you were going away and all. . . . Or maybe, you were just busy . . . would you come for Jason and me like you promised?"

Ma stumbled. "I—I'd say yes. But maybe, maybe I'd be having a rough time. There could be lots of reasons." She brushed some imaginary dust off her shirt. She finally said, "I don't know, honey. It's so hard to say."

"Ma."

"Hmm?"

"You go along with how Daddy treats us?"

"No. But um . . ." Ma shook her head, nervously.

"Do I have to go with him next time? I don't want to."

"Your father loves you."

"I know. But I want to do something else next Saturday," I said, trying to think of something in case she asked me what.

She said, "We'll see." She pinched my cheek and tugged my braid. It didn't hurt. She got up and said, "Good night."

She turned off the light over my bed. Her body melted

into the darkness. I felt around for her in the dark. Even in the worst times, Ma was warm and nearby.

"What?" She squeezed my hand.

It's been a long time since I heard fighting, yelling, crying, and doors slamming in the middle of the night. Only Jason's steady breathing filled the room. The quiet was so loud, it made me dizzy. It was never this peaceful when Daddy was around.

"What, honey? It's late."

"Oh, nothing. I was just wondering. What can I tell everybody about why I was absent?"

Ma laughed. "The truth. What else?" She asked as though she suspected I was up to something.

"No. Not the truth. No way."

Ma laughed again and said, "Good night, now."

The next few days were long and boring. So when Thursday morning came, I rushed out of the house into warm sunshine.

Rhonda was walking up the block. I called her, but when she saw it was me, she kept on walking. I ran to catch up with her. I was out of breath.

"Leave me alone," she said angrily. She was loaded down with books and stuff, just like me.

"Nobody's bothering you," I said, and sucked my teeth.

She rolled her eyes. I didn't care if she was acting snooty. I had something important to talk over with her.

"Listen a minute, will you?" She stared straight ahead. She didn't tell me to get lost or anything, so I said, "I thought maybe we should tell the kids we had a twenty-four hour virus. You know, instead of being suspended and all."

"Boy, a twenty-four hour virus? For three days?" She gave me her famous disgusted look. Suddenly, her eyes brightened, and she grinned.

I nodded. "Wait. A twenty-four hour virus with . . ." Rhonda didn't let me finish.

She began jumping up and down with excitement and hitting on me, like it was her idea. "I know. I know. A twenty-four hour virus with . . . forty-eight hours' worth of complications." The last part we said together.

In a very mysterious voice, I added, "The worst part is . . . it's deadly contagious."

She winced.

"That'll keep them from bugging us for awhile."

"Probably forever," Rhonda said sadly.

"We'll think of something else later. Okay?"

It was as if we were almost friends, sharing this secret joke. Now we've shared two things. It seems like just two anyway. Maybe later there'll be more.

"Okay," she said. "Now I can go back to being the best student in the class."

I didn't say that Nereida was better than her. I said, "Yeah." I smiled. She smiled back. It felt good. And wouldn't you know that for the rest of the way to school, we fussed over who caught the virus from who.

But we walked into the school yard together. Just like friends.